Henry Varley

The Christian Ambassador

Henry Varley

The Christian Ambassador

ISBN/EAN: 9783741123139

Manufactured in Europe, USA, Canada, Australia, Japa

Cover: Foto ©Andreas Hilbeck / pixelio.de

Manufactured and distributed by brebook publishing software
(www.brebook.com)

Henry Varley

The Christian Ambassador

THE

CHRISTIAN AMBASSADOR

AND OTHER

ADDRESSES,

BY

HENRY VARLEY,

WITH AN

INTRODUCTION, BY REV. STEPHEN H. TYNG, Jr., D. D.

WILLARD TRACT REPOSITORY,
Deacon Hill Place, Boston.
No. 239 Fourth Avenue, New York.
Shaftesbury Hall, Toronto, Canada.

INTRODUCTION.

HENRY VARLEY, the English evangelist, was born in Tattershall, Lincolnshire, England, in the year 1835. At the age of fifteen he was born again, of water and of the Spirit, under the ministrations of the Rev. Baptist Noel. Two years later he went to Australia, where he remained three years ; but during this period, though diligent in business, his fervent spirit was also intent on serving the Lord in the more direct methods of evangelistic work. On his return to London, however, the providence of God seemed to indicate that he should pursue for a time longer his secular avocation, (he had kept a meat-market in Australia,) and he embraced the new business opportunity, not without many longings for employment more congenial to the new spirit and purpose that had filled his heart since the time of his conversion. He has often since that time found cause to thank the all-wise Master, that he was appointed to bear witness as a business man among business men,

to the transforming and supporting power of God's grace
in the Gospel.

About the year 1860, Mr. Varley became specially
interested in the Kensington Potteries School, of which
he became Superintendent. His preaching there on
Sunday evenings, led finally to the building of the West
London Tabernacle, at St. James' Square, Nottinghill,
which, from the time of its opening, was regularly filled
by people anxious to listen to his interpretations of the
Word of God. The church that grew out of these
labors, is a practical embodiment of his belief, that true
spiritual union is not the result of any denominational
code, ritual, or polity, but rather the result of the Holy
Spirit's work in every living member of Christ's body.
Mr. Varley evidently believes in the unity of the Spirit,
as maintained by the power and grace of God in the
hearts of Christians, and cares but little for the minor
diversities that characterize the real Church of Christ.

His labors have been remarkable in two important
respects. First, they have been the labors of a lay evangelist. He has presented himself to men as a Christian
business man, too solicitous for their welfare in the life
to come, to be selfishly and wholly absorbed in his own
concerns in this. His well-known probity and simplicity
in secular affairs, has emphasized his influence upon the
platform. The hundreds of invitations that have poured
in upon him from different parts of England during the
last five years, are significant of a general need as well as
of a popular demand. The people needed to hear the

gospel according to the fresh conceptions of one of their own number; to hear just such a simple, direct exposition of Scriptural truth as a tradesman, led by the Spirit of God, would make to his fellows. In the variety of ministrations ordained by God, the mission of the evangelist had been neglected ; and when the instrument was raised up by God, the opportunity for its use became suddenly manifest.

The call for Mr. Varley's labors has also been attested by the most conclusive of all events, the blessing of God in the bringing of men to repentance and faith. On this one fact alone rests the complete justification of his course. Call it an exception, an innovation, provisional, — the answer is, "*And believers were the more added to the Lord, multitudes both of men and women.*" The work of this evangelist has been sealed by the outpouring of that Holy Spirit of promise, against the diverse operations of which no Christian may speak a word. Fearful indeed would be the responsibility of the Christian pastor who should say to such a messenger of Christ, I cannot bid you God-speed.

Of Mr. Varley's recent visit to this country, I have scarcely left room to speak in terms befitting the cordial interest awakened in the minds of those ministerial brethren, of various denominations, who shared with me the opportunity of hearing him. The simplicity and directness of his expositions of Scripture, the vividness of his illustrations, the vigor of his personal appeals, may be judged of somewhat, by the contents of this volume ; but no reader can supply the impressions made by voice and manner, by emphasis and tone, and it was these impressions that gave insight as to his calm resting upon God for strength and guidance, and noble longing for success *as a servant of Jesus Christ.* That this beloved brother may never miss for one moment the abiding Christ, who has been his strength and glory thus far, is the prayer of his grateful fellow-worker in the gospel,

S. H. TYNG, JR.

NEW YORK, NOVEMBER 1, 1875.

CONTENTS.

THE

CHRISTIAN AMBASSADOR.

II CORINTHIANS v. 20.

NOW THEN WE ARE AMBASSADORS FOR CHRIST, AS THOUGH GOD
DID BESEECH YOU BY US : WE PRAY YOU IN CHRIST'S STEAD,
BE YE RECONCILED TO GOD.

I WILL deal first of all with the term here
expressed by the word *Ambassador.* You all
know an ambassador is one who is sent by the
country wherein he dwells — usually some distinguished man — to represent the court of the country
from whence he comes to some neighboring nation.
Observe this, we, in England, don't send an ambassador to Canada from the Imperial Government,
for the simple reason that Canada represents a
colony. At present the world is under the rule of
God's great opponent, the devil; the world is not
now subject to God, and will not be until Christ
comes, whose right it is to reign ; meanwhile the
Lord sends ambassadors. England sends ambassadors to France, Italy and Austria, on the very

ground that these are independent governments, and which are in turn represented by ambassadors so acting.

Now, I want you to understand that I have no sympathy with distinctions among Christians. I don't want to do anything or assume any position that would lead one to suppose that I was separate from my fellow men. I do dislike anything that savors of what is expressed by the word *Priest*—in fact anything like affected superiority; yet I gladly recognize the power for good of the great minds that have gone before, and I have listened to their majestic words ; and I thank God, nevertheless, that we have these treasures in earthen vessels, but the excellency of the power is of God and not of us. O how true is it said by one of our poets, that "one touch of nature makes the whole world kin." I thank God for trials ; to know what it is to buffet with vulgar manhood—and I have no small share in the busy scenes of our urgent London life—and more than all, I do thank God that He has put me in trust, and accepted me as an ambassador of Christ to speak to you to-night.

I do affirm that I strive every morning in coming out of my room to pray that my commission be straight from the throne of God. My citizenship is neither Toronto nor London, it is heaven, according to the authority of that Word; therefore I have a perfect right to come down from the presence of the great King, morning after morning, with the spirit of the better country marking my entire life, with the language of that country on my tongue, with the laws of that country to administer wheresoever I can — to beseech my fellow men, or, as my text puts it, to "pray you in Christ's stead to be reconciled unto God" to-night. In all the earnest purpose of my soul, I come to you and tell you that I am an ambassador of the Great King.

Earthly potentates may have their distinguished representatives, but oh, brethren, I do thank God that it is written, "Our sufficiency is of God." I come to act as one of His ambassadors ; *my* embassage is one of peace. I come to make known unto you, something of the laws of my royal Master — something of His feelings towards you. I come to tell you that He is no abstraction, living at an infinite distance from you, without any interest in your welfare. I come to bring the burden of my embassage, and I thank His precious name that I may represent Him to you to-night in the character of the Father, whose boundless love is only co-extensive with eternity itself.

Come with me to-night into yonder cottage, standing near the sea-coast. There sits working at her needle the form of a mother some fifty years of age. I approach her gently and lay my hand on her shoulder and say, " Sister, bear with a stranger speaking to you; have you not a son?" Oh, how my question stirs her heart; how those poor blue eyes look out of their depths into mine. She says, "I have, do you know anything about him?" I say, "Yes." This youth went away from his mother twenty years before, and well nigh broke that

mother's heart.   How she has waited long for
tidings of him.   I want you to suppose that I could
bring that boy from behind the door, and then you
could fancy the thin arms of that mother being
wrapt about him.   Her affection is all engrossing.
She does not ask, "Is my boy's character changed?"
She does not wait for that, but sees him before his
sin.   My brethren, that is just what my great Lord
does.   He deprecates sin, yet He does not send me
with an embassage of fault-finding to night.   "If
thou knewest the gift of God, and who it is that
saith to thee, Give Me to drink; thou wouldest have
asked of Him, and He would have given thee living
water."

An ambassador not only represents the court of
his country, but represents also the commerce of
that country.   I am here to-night to represent the
commerce of the blessed God, and I tell you He
has loaded these hands with blessings and charged
these lips with testimony concerning you.   I pray
Him to give me right words, and the power to
properly speak and impress them upon your hearts.
Great as my Master is, He is full of love, but sin is
an abomination to Him.   My brother, if you persist
in drunkenness, if you persist in appetite, if you
persist in the companionship of the harlot, if you
persist in unbelief, or in keeping away from the
love of God, the time is coming when your waywardness will lead you to the brink of that fearful
precipice, which will effectually shut you out from
God, and bring about that terrible darkness in

which it shall be said, " My feet stumbled upon the dark mountains."

Such a scene I have before me now. A young man — a member of our church — once came to me to go and see a man in distress of soul. I went. When I entered his room, he was walking about as though he had never been so strong in his life. Though scarcely understanding it, I questioned him about his soul's concern. He said, " I don't want to see you ; they tell me I am going to die. I won't die," and he paced about the room violently. But it was only too surely known by his relatives that he had contracted some terrible disease, and had come home with an affection of the throat which was actually choking him. The physicians said he could not live longer than two o'clock in the morning. He just went about the room half mad, shouting, " I won't die, I won't die," but death with his ominous finger beckoned him to the tomb, and at two o'clock he died !

Oh, beloved friends, it is a dreadful thing to trifle with sin. It was sin that brought Jesus Christ from His throne. He came to put it away. I tell you, brethren, that there is not a man, woman or child in this room to-night, for whom the Lord Jesus did not die. Then perhaps some one says, " If the Lord Jesus died for me I shall be saved !" Not necessarily. Though Christ was a sacrifice for sin, yet I tell you that if you reject Him, His sacrifice cannot deal with that sin in its very nature. What you will be condemned for is this — not because you have been a drunkard, or unclean, but

the main count of the indictment will be, that
though God offered you life in Christ, you spurned
it contemptuously. He offered you a free and full
pardon, an entire acquittal of your guilt, and you
say, 'I care not for it, I would rather have my sin
than God's testimony.' Oh, brethren, I would that
many of you would wake up and thank God for
sending the message of peace to us. Thanks be to
God for His unspeakable gift.

I come here to-night from my Father in heaven,
with the gift of His own dear Son to you, and I
want you to realize that you have a perfect right to
Christ. I would say to the drunkard, "Here, take
Christ as you are, take Him now." I never expect
to see you turn away from sin until you get hold of
Christ.   There is not a man here that I would ask
to give up the seeming and false pleasures of the
world until the Spirit of the Lord has rested upon
him.   May you receive Him into your hearts to-
night, and He will break the bonds that bind you,
and set you free.   They smiled at me one evening
in Shaftesbury Hall, when I mentioned an incident
about a street-crossing sweeper in Dublin.   A
solicitor came to him one day, and looking into his
face, asked if his name was so and so.   The sweeper
replied it was.   "Then," said the lawyer, "a client
of ours has died and left you twenty thousand
pounds."   The sweeper immediately flung the
broom over to the farther side of the street, and
said he would never use it any more.   I want you
to lay hold of Christ, and then you can fling away
your sins and not until then.   He exhorts you to

come to Him. Mark these words: "To wit, that God was in Christ, reconciling the world unto Himself, not imputing their trespasses unto them; and hath committed unto us the word of reconciliation."

Here, brethren, bear with me. You will find numbers of men in this city who speak about the doctrine of Christ as though it was some bloody sacrifice. They scoff at the glorious doctrine of the atonement — the great central lesson of the New Testament. God was the sufferer. Mark what I say. He it was who endured the wrath—it was He who magnified the law and made it honorable. Mark what St. Paul says in Acts, 20th chapter, "Take heed therefore unto yourselves, and to all the flock, over which the Holy Ghost hath made you overseers, to feed the church of God, which He hath purchased with His own blood." Oh, brethren, again I entreat you to remember it was the Father in the Son. What! Vindicating a wrong — the crucifixion was an outrage on the principles of justice! No, Sir. Suppose that I have committed some terrible crime in Canada, and as the result of that crime I had to forfeit my life. I am lying in one of your prisons under sentence of death. You could understand our beloved Queen, with her womanly heart full of pitying love towards me, as one of her subjects, — and the Prince of Wales sharing that love, — on his royal mother's behalf delaying the execution of the sentence. He says, "Next to the Queen I am the embodiment of the law, by virtue of my position as chiefest magistrate.

Now I am prepared to take the place of my subject,
let *me* die, that poor Henry Varley may go free.
Let the law take effect on me."

The Prince of Wales dying for me is substantially
the death accepted in the place of my own. Behold
the man loved by his prince to this extent that he
died for him. See the law magnified in the person
of him who is its chief representative. And even
so, the Lord Jesus Christ, the great representative
of the law, has come from heaven, and in His own
body bore our sins on the tree. Receive this testimony, for it is your birthright — receive it, for it is
liberty to the captive. It is the opening of the
prison doors to them that are bound. Is Jesus
Christ going to die for you? No, you answer, His
death is an accomplished fact. If you believe to-
night that Jesus died for you, sing aloud, shout and
say, " I am made free by the death of my Prince,"
and then, walking with your head erect, you say,
" Put me, if you will, in that condemned cell and
put chains on my legs, I don't care, I have a
reprieve in the Queen's name;" and I will say to
the jailor, " Knock off those manacles, unloosen
that door, I won't stop here." "But you are a
criminal!" " Never mind, I have a reprieve, here
it is." " Now then, we are ambassadors for Christ,
as though God did beseech you by us, be ye
reconciled to God."

Oh, my dear brethren, remember that sin is put
away by the sacrifice of Christ. Oh, brother, believe it; sinner, receive it. Christ Jesus has died,
and you and I who believe in Him are free. Mark

you, the gospel does not tell you to go and break off some habit that you are powerless to control until you have the Saviour's power in your heart. My brother, I would not cheat you — take Christ ; for the Spirit of my Master says He came to give liberty to the captive and unbar the prison doors. Do we, I wonder, regard sufficiently the awfulness of the gospel truth wherein we are told that the final day will witness those who reject Christ condemned, and those who believe on Him accepted and saved ! Faith in Christ will break forever that association with Adam, so that you can take your place and say, ' I am not under the dominion of the law, I am united to Christ, and just as surely as Christ lives, I shall live also.'

The man who makes Christianity a mere system of morals, confesses his want of faith in the gospel, for " if any man be in Christ he is a new creature, old things have passed away and behold all things have become new." Suppose a man in business in this city gets into difficulties and is forced to call his creditors together, and in the height of his perplexity a friend turns up, who not only volunteers to pay every farthing, but supplies fresh capital to start again. So long as these creditors have been paid, no matter by whom, that business man can go out into the streets and no creditor can say a word. Now, if sin comes and enters a claim, or if death comes and says, " I have a claim upon you," I say death is dishonest. Listen to Christ's own words, " I am the resurrection and the life : He that believeth on Me, though he were dead, yet shall he live, and whosoever liveth and believeth in Me shall never die."

Let me venture to read to you a letter that I brought with me from England, written by a physician who lives in Boston, Lincolnshire. "My dear Sir : — I presume you are accustomed to receive letters from persons about whom you know very little. From the very brief interview I had with you, I cannot think that you will remember me, but I feel it to be my duty to tell you what great things the Lord has done for me, and how greatly He has blessed your ministrations unto me. I came home to Boston about two months ago, thoroughly broken down through repeated failures, and for fourteen years I have been struggling with appetite and an insatiable thirst for alcoholic drinks. I fell into that powerlessness that possesses one who is addicted to intemperate habits. Many times I thought I would be free, and signed pledges, formed resolutions, made promises — in fact all the useless and lame methods to free myself from the power of the enemy I had adopted. Some eight years ago I went away to South Africa, where I hoped to reform my habits, but all to no purpose. Time would fail me to tell you the experiences of the last fifteen years. . . . How I remember a sermon that you preached from these words : ' I am crucified with Christ ; nevertheless I live, yet not I, but Christ liveth in me ; and the life which I now live in the flesh I live by the faith of the Son of God, who loved me and gave Himself for me.' So through God's Spirit I was brought to Him. My heart from that day to this has experienced almost uninterrupted peace and joy such as I never knew before."

This freedom is open for all, inasmuch as Christ died for all. I am not going to ask you to reform yourselves. I have seen enough of that miserable failure. "Therefore if any man be in Christ he is a new creature ; old things are passed away, behold all things are become new." The reason that many a man is full of prejudice against the gospel, is just because his understanding is utterly in the dark about it. Some think that to be a Christian is to take hold of a system of morals which will be constantly restraining him in his life. It is nothing of the kind. It is a great, generous life inside you, which developes when you become a believer in Christ. "We are ambassadors for Christ, as though God did beseech you by us, we pray you in Christ's stead be ye reconciled to God."

When in Dublin, some three years ago, a young man came to me and said, "Dear Sir, I am so glad to see you; last time you were here, only a few months ago, I experienced the *great pass.*" I said, "What do you mean?" He then repeated the twenty-fourth verse, fifth chapter of John, "Verily, verily, I say unto you, he that heareth My word and believeth on Him that sent Me, hath everlasting life and shall not come into condemnation, *but is passed from death unto life.*" He said, "That is the great pass I refer to, sir." Like the friend who not only pays your debts but backs you with half a million dollars to live upon, the Lord is not

only merciful to you in putting away your sins —
He is not only doing that, but He is giving you
new life. It is not a little brief time of thirty, fifty
or seventy uncertain years before us, but it is the
great Master who upholds·yonder sun and has kept
it full of light for sixty thousand years — perhaps
six hundred thousand years, for all I know. Christ
is omniscient, the Christian's beacon. "The Lord
is my light and my salvation."

There is not a young man here to-night, I don't
care how ignorant or stupid he may be, who, if
he accept the message of the Master, may not join
the holy throng of ransomed spirits. I bring you
the free gift of God, without money and without
price. He can wrap up His influence for good in
your hearts, just as He can wrap up an oak in an
acorn. The Christianity of the Gospel compels a
man to say, "I have done with anxiety, for I know
the Lord will never forsake me." The idea of sane
men daring to affirm that they can get more out
of other things than they can get out of Christ!
Remember, salvation is God's gift — not a poor
uncertain thing, fraught with all the doubts that
beset human affairs! Oh, the joy that is in store
for sinners everywhere, if they would only accept of it. I know a young man in London, that
came into a meeting of Christians, and was
astounded at the genial and generous life maintained. He had imagined a life without energy,
without activity, but did not find it so. Oh, beloved
brethren, I beg of you to disabuse your minds of

that false idea of Christianity and choose the better part at once.

Oh, that I had the power of entering into this as though God did beseech you, and so that God would uplift the veil of darkness from your eyes that you might see the phases of His character. God's omnipresence allows the whole mechanism of the material universe to go on. I have sometimes believed that one reason that God has put the material universe under laws from which there is no appeal, save by His sovereign power, is, that He may have His hands free for the needs of the great family of men, and diffuse the great energies of His power for the benefit of the human race. Perhaps some of you are like others that I have known, just a bundle of dogmas, instead of recognizing over and above all these, the glorious foundation of life. Get out of this wretched road and go in yonder, that you may understand the meaning of what He said to the woman at the well, "Whosoever drinketh of this water, shall thirst again ; but whosoever drinketh of the water that I shall give him shall never thirst, but the water that I shall give him shall be in him a well of water springing up into everlasting life."

My Master cannot bear that you should die. Again I repeat to you — perhaps the largest assembly of young men ever brought together in Canada — why will you turn a deaf ear to His entreaties ? Brethren, I lose sight of myself, forgetting any other than the great King — He beseeches you, by that uplifted Christ, why will ye

2

die! He asks you to come and believe. If God
had said to me, "Henry Varley, I must make a
condition of moral excellence," there would have
been the devil's saving clause. Don't let the devil
cheat you — he is ever watching for plausible ex-
cuses. Have faith in God and exercise it. You
take a cheque from a merchant on the faith that
funds are provided for it. At the table you have
implicit faith that the cook has not poisoned the
food. I am going to Niagara to-morrow; what
if I should say to the man of whom I buy my ticket,
"I won't have it, for I have no faith that this line
leads to Niagara." Sincere reliance upon God's
promises and consistent observance of His laws,
will ensure the kingdom of heaven. I care not of
what color or nationality you may be,—God is just
and the justifier of him that believes in Christ
Jesus. A believer in Jesus is a man that is not
condemned. Ah, my brethren, there is such a
depth of love that we cannot know much about it.
Oh, that I could get my little cup full, deep in the
great ocean of His love.

Oh, that you had known this day of visitation and
this day of grace, when the offer of complete pardon
from the Throne of Grace is put into your hands—
when the offer of the boundless love of Christ is
given to you without money and without price. We
pray you in Christ's stead, that you may not reject
His offer. He knows what an awful hell you are
meriting by your sin. The Saviour pleads with
you and for you, and sheds His benign influence
over transgressing humanity like crystal streams

that radiate from a fountain. The sacred stream
of His power puts out the fever fires of sin. Oh!
but this water of life is refreshing, cleansing and
purifying ; take it, accept this blessed river that
God gives to His people, as it comes rippling from
the hill-sides of Jehovah's boundless love—a fit
emblem of Jesus. I charge you reject it not. Un-
burden your souls to the Redeemer, and listen to
His pleading through His weak servant who will
soon leave you. The ambassador leaves you, but
you have many zealous, earnest brethren among
you, to whom I hope you will confide your souls'
burdens. There is a time in the history of nations,
when a declaration of war is made and the withdrawal of the ambassador immediately precedes the
appeal to arms. I believe, if this Word is true, that
we are on the eve of the withdrawal of His ambassadors, and then you know what follows. In that
dark hour there will be none to speak of the love
of Jesus — the ambassadors will be withdrawn.

Oh God, again I cry on behalf of my indifferent
brethren ; Thou knowest our yearning hearts cannot bear the rejection of Christ; Thou knowest
that indifference and delay are fatal. Do Thou
awaken the careless, arouse the slumberer, and
warn the scoffer. I hope I have only spoken in
your city as one in earnest. Mark you yonder
glaring red light on the prairie — it is on fire.
Would you account me a fool because I warn the
occupant of that wooden building of his danger —
because I say, Fight fire with fire, as he gathers and
fires a circle of grass about him, and when the

devouring fiend comes on he passes unscathed through it all! Just so, I come to warn you as an ambassador from God. I have seen something of the glory of heaven and heard the swell of its rapturous music, where former things have passed away, where sin is not and where death has no place. "Now then, we are ambassadors for Christ, as though God did beseech you by us, we pray you in Christ's stead, be ye reconciled to God." When once you have accepted the message and yielded to the entreaty of the ambassadors, the vital force of Christ's love will shield you against the common enemy, and cause a warm and generous blood to start through the veins of that system, no longer weak, but strong. May the lessons of other men's lives and the solemn injunctions once more repeated, sink deeper and deeper into your hearts, and bear fruit in a purer life and increased devotion to the Saviour, for Christ's sake. AMEN.

THE

SIN OF UNBELIEF.

—◦◦⟩⊙⟨◦◦—

HEBREWS III. 18.

AND TO WHOM SWARE HE THAT THEY SHOULD NOT ENTER INTO
HIS REST, BUT TO THEM THAT BELIEVED NOT?

WE are called in the Scripture, " The children
of faith," or, " the children of the promise,"
our only heritage being that of " the exceeding great and precious promises." The Christian differs from the worldling in this respect, that
while the worldling lives upon himself and upon
the things by which he is surrounded, the Christian
believes that " man shall not live by bread alone,
but by every word that proceedeth out of the
mouth of God." Hence, it is of the highest importance to us to be constantly listening to what the
Lord says : and if, as the liturgy of the Church of
England so beautifully expresses it, we do " mark,
learn, and inwardly digest " the word, we shall have
realized in us the fulfillment of that beautiful verse,
the second of the fifty-fifth chapter of Isaiah. You

will observe that the Lord is here speaking to His children, " Hearken diligently unto Me, and eat ye that which is good, and let your soul delight itself in fatness." Now, that is just one of many striking passages I might give, illustrative of our position as "the children of promise." Practically, our life is a feeding upon the truth of God, from morning to night, and he most fully carries out this idea who can say, " I have esteemed the words of Thy mouth more than my necessary food."

By way of illustration, let me suppose that instead of standing before you in physical vigor and health, I were emaciated and feeble. I can understand your kind expressions of regret at my apparent weakness. I account for it by telling you that for a week I have not tasted food. Why, you would immediately regret that you had not known of my necessities, which you would have hastened to relieve. "Oh !" I should say, " there was abundance before me, but I did not choose to eat." Then your sympathy would be changed into deserved censure. Now, I believe that to be the case with numbers of Christians to-day ; there is plenty provided, but they will not take it ; and let me say to you, if you practically set aside the eating of this bread, — the Word of God, — as the Lord liveth, you will spend your years saying, " My leanness, my leanness."

And now, let me show you, that when we are converted to God, faith begins to work. "Trust," in the Old Testament, and "faith," in the New Testament, are synonymous terms. "They that

trust in the Lord, shall be as Mount Zion, which
may not be removed, but standeth fast for ever."
That will give you the Old Testament testimony to
the importance of this principle, which God sets in
operation in our souls when we are first converted ;
and I press this upon you, because there is danger
of forgetting that the same principle of faith which
enabled us to apprehend Jesus, as our Saviour, is
to be the capital with which we are ever after to
work. Faith is to be exercised all along the line
of our life. Its best analogy I believe is found in
the act of breathing. If this be suspended for any
lengthened period in the natural body, death en-
sues ; and the spiritual life can only be maintained
by faith ; for " The just shall live by faith."

The opposite of faith is unbelief, and I want now
to show you the importance of crushing out this
terrible sin. A brother minister observed to me,
during a conference we were holding in London :—
" One thing is evident ; that numbers of you seem,
within a few months, to have come into possession
of a great accession of spiritual power. I am full
of interest on this subject. I long for it, need it,
and see what an advantage it would be to me ; but
what am I to do ?" My reply was, " Exercise faith
in God." " Well, what do you mean by that ?"
" Simply," I replied, " that, at this very moment,
you believe that you really have all that God has
promised in Christ,—fullness of joy, fullness of the
Holy Ghost,—in a word, all that is comprehended
in ' God's unspeakable gift,' because He makes no
reservation." He answered, " I don't feel that ; I

feel as empty as possible." "For that very reason,"
said I, "do I ask you to exercise faith. You have
been for years pleading with awakened souls to
look away from their own feelings, and trust to
God's stated fact of Christ as their Saviour, and to
turn away from the process of introspection and
self-examination, and believe God's word ; and now
that I ask you to turn away from feelings, and
believe that you have all fullness of joy and peace
in Christ, you refuse. It is the old sin, the mon-
strous sin of unbelief."

I spoke strongly as I do now to you, because for
years I myself looked on this terrible sin as my
infirmity, thinking I was to be pitied for it ; where-
as, now I view it as that from which I would recoil
with the same horror as from drunkenness. Bear
with me, when I say you have no business to continue under the control of this sin ; no right to
indulge it. It is the parent of all other sin, and
must ever be placed in the front of offending, as a
thing to be intensely hated. I was very much
struck with an illustration of this which I heard
lately. A youth, the son of a farmer, was in the
habit of jumping across a brook which separated a
certain field from the house ; on one occasion,
coming with a rapid run to this brook, the rapidity
of his pace prevented his seeing, until too late to
stop himself, a black snake coiled up at his feet.
He trod on it, and as it was providentially asleep,
he reached the other side in safety ; but never
could he forget the horror of feeling the cold slime
of the reptile against his bare foot. He said : " I

cried, God help me." And so, let each of us say, "God help us from this awful sin."

I have no hope as touching the enlargement of your souls, until this sin is dealt with. Now, nothing can be more important than to have the testimony of God's word on this point; and I think, that in the experience of the children of Israel, we have the strongest illustration of the terrible power of unbelief. This it was which kept the children of Israel forty years out of their promised inheritance. Their toilsome wanderings had formed no part of God's plan. No; redemption from the house of bondage was immediately to be supplemented by entrance into Canaan. It had not been God's design to let their carcases fall in the wilderness, until every man of that unbelieving generation had perished. I remember hearing a sermon, in which it was said that the children of Israel, being little better than slaves when they left Egypt, required the forty years in the wilderness to prepare them for the promised land; missing altogether the important point, that they actually sank into dishonored graves, so that only their children went into the land.

When this first engaged my attention, I cannot tell you the wondrous blessing it was to me. Let me substantiate this serious statement from the word of God. First, turn to the seventy-eighth Psalm, and read it carefully. In the fourth verse note, "We will not hide them," speaking of the things of God, "from their children, showing to the generation to come, the praises of the Lord, and

His strength, and His wonderful works that He hath done." Again, at the seventh verse, "That they might set their hope in God, and not forget the works of God, but keep His commandments." In the tenth verse, "They kept not the covenant of God, and refused to walk in His law ; and forgat His works, and His wonders that He had showed them. Marvellous things did He in the sight of their fathers, in the land of Egypt, in the field of Zoan." And so on, to the end of the Psalm. And again, I ask you to read the one hundred and sixth Psalm, from beginning to end, as a further proof of the abomination of the sin of unbelief.

Come back with me now, to the book of Numbers, where you will find such testimony as, I pray God, may prove to many the life-long blessing it was to me. In the thirteenth and fourteenth chapters of that book you will find these words* : — "And Moses sent them" (the heads of the tribes) "to spy out the land of Canaan, and said unto them, Get you up this way southward, and go up into the mountain : and see the land, what it is ; and the people that dwelleth therein, whether they be strong or weak, few or many ; and what the land is that they dwell in, whether it be good or bad ; and what cities they be that they dwell in, whether in tents, or in strong holds ; and what the land is, whether it be fat or lean, whether there be wood therein, or not. And be ye of good courage, and bring of the fruit of the land." Now, you may form some idea of the terrible straits to which

---

* Chapter 13, verse 17.

Moses, the servant of God, was reduced, when he had to put these particulars before these men, in order to induce them to go and spy out the land. God had promised it to them,— He had said it was a land flowing with milk and honey, yet they "thought scorn of that pleasant land." Then observe, "And they returned from searching of the land after forty days. And they went and came to Moses, and to Aaron, and to all the congregation of the children of Israel, * * * and brought back word unto them, and unto all the congregation, and showed them the fruit of the land. And they told him, and said, We came unto the land whither thou sentest us, and surely it floweth with milk and honey ; and this is the fruit of it. Nevertheless the people be strong that dwell in the land, and the cities are walled, and very great; and moreover we saw the children of Anak there. * * * And Caleb stilled the people before Moses, and said, Let us go up at once, and possess it, for we are well able to overcome it."

I should not wonder if there were some here to-day who, in speaking of the abundance of blessing in what is sometimes called, (though I do not like the phrase,) the higher Christian life, would say to me, "There are difficulties in the way that cannot be overcome." So said unbelief concerning Canaan. So said not faith! Faith said, and it says to-day, "Let us go up and possess it, for we are well able to overcome it." "But the men that went up with him said, We be not able to go up against the people ; for they are stronger than we." That is the mischief. So long as you believe your spiritual enemies are stronger than you are, so long you must be depressed and brought down ; so long as you do not sing faith's triumphant song, ' Greater is He that is on our part, than all that are against us,' you must know this miserable depression. And now notice one of the grandest statements ever made in proof of the miserableness of unbelief. '· They brought up an evil report of the land which they had searched, unto the children of Israel, say-ing, The land, through which we have gone to search it, is a land that eateth up the inhabitants thereof ; and all the people that we saw in it, are men of a great stature." They did not hesitate to tell a lie in the presence of God. "And there we saw the giants." Of course ; — unbelief is always seeing them ; did you ever know an unbeliever who was not looking at giants? "The sons of Anak, which come of the giants, and we were," — I com-mend to you, and especially to my clerical brethren, this last clause, "And we were, in our own sight, as grasshoppers." I do not object to that, — the smaller we are in our own sight the better, — but then comes the cowardice of unbelief, "And so we were in their sight." Not only have they a lowly estimate of themselves, but they voluntarily go over to the enemies' side. "And so we were in their sight." Oh ! let us be careful of this abomin-able sin of unbelief.

Now, look at the fourteenth chapter, twenty-second verse, "Because all those men which have seen my glory, and my miracles, which I did in

Egypt, and in the wilderness, and have tempted me now these ten times, and have not hearkened unto my voice,"—look at God's forbearance there,—"these ten times." Now I want you thoughtfully to notice that these words were spoken not fifteen months after the redemption from Egypt,—"Surely they shall not see the land which I sware unto their fathers, neither shall any of them that provoked me see it; but my servant Caleb, because he had another spirit with him, and hath followed me fully, him will I bring into the land whereinto he went; and his seed shall possess it. * * * And the Lord spake unto Moses and unto Aaron, saying, How long shall I bear with this evil congregation, which murmur against Me? I have heard the murmurings of the children of Israel, which they murmur against me. Say unto them,"—Oh! if I am speaking to unbelieving Christians here, I would repeat it in God's name to every one of you in solemn, tender, brotherly affection,—"Your carcases shall fall in this wilderness, and all that were numbered of you, according to your whole number, from twenty years old and upward, which have murmured against me, doubtless ye shall not come into the land, concerning which I sware to make you dwell therein, save Caleb, the son of Jephunneh, and Joshua the son of Nun. But your little ones, which ye said should be a prey, them will I bring in, and they shall know the land which ye have despised. But as for you, your carcases, they shall fall in this wilderness. And your children shall wander in the wilderness forty years,

2*

and bear your whoredoms, until your carcases be
wasted in the wilderness. After the number of
the days in which ye searched the land, even forty
days, each day for a year, shall ye bear your iniquities, even forty years, and ye shall know my breach
of promise," or, as it is in the margin, "the alter-
ing of my purpose."

Again, I say, God had never designed that this
redeemed people should die in the wilderness.
Now, why do I press this? Because, beloved
friends, that land of Canaan, the land flowing with
milk and honey, was not typical of heaven only, or
primarily. It typifies our life in Christ. We enter
into Him, as into our land of promise, and we find
it a land that yields its supplies without labor on
our part. Mark this, — it is a land that *flows* with
milk and honey. Entering into it, we may say, " I
have all, and abound, being full." ' My God hath
supplied all my need.' We grasp the title-deed of
the Eternal One, and say, " All things are mine,
for I am Christ's, and Christ is God's." Oh!
beloved friends, let not this abominable sin of
unbelief continue to wither, blight and curse your
characters, until, perchance, it may be said of you
as of the Corinthians, " For this cause many are
weak and sickly among you, and many sleep." I
think, of all the desperate sins which the child of
God can commit, the worst is to go on disbelieving
God. To illustrate: I fancy my eldest boy, — a
youth of fifteen, now in India, but soon to return,—
I fancy him entering my study and saying, " I am
sorry, father, to tell you, but I really cannot believe

a word you say. I know it is my infirmity, and
you will pity, not blame me for it." Think how
such language would wound a father's heart! Oh!
brethren, in the Master's name I beseech you be
believing believers of every Word of God.

And now let us notice another verse or two. In
the thirty-fifth verse of this chapter, "I the Lord
have said, I will surely do it unto all this evil congregation, that are gathered together against me; in
this wilderness they shall be consumed, and there
shall they die;" and this because they brought an
evil report of that land. I think of our Father
coming quietly to each of us, as we sit here, and
saying, "My child, are you satisfied with Jesus? At
an infinite cost to Myself I sent Him, with His beautiful, magnificent life. I gave it you out of the fullness of this boundless love of Mine. Are you satisfied with it? Do you find its dignity suitable to
you? Does its sweetness permeate your whole
being? Does it make your home-life beautiful?
Is it a calm, peaceful, gentle life, helping you to
suffer long, and be kind? Are you slow to receive
evil thoughts? Do you find that the instincts of
that life in you, lead to this: 'Seeing ye have purified your souls in obeying the truth, through the
Spirit, unto unfeigned love of the brethren, see that
ye love one another with a pure heart fervently.'"
Does that great, dignified life permeate with its
excellence every part of your being? For it is
written, 'He that believeth on me, out of his belly
shall flow rivers of living water.' I would call
your attention, before I have done, to the testi-

mony found in the Epistle to the Hebrews on this very point. In the third chapter and seventh verse you will find these words : "Wherefore, as the Holy Ghost saith, To-day, if ye will hear His voice ;" and I want you to notice that expression, "to-day," for, I think, it occurs no less than six or seven times in the next few verses. It is as though our Father should say to us, "My children, you have disbelieved me until now, but to-day, if you will hear my voice, I will obliterate the past."

May He thus speak with power to many among us now. "Harden not your hearts, *as in the provocation.*" What ! my dear friends, shall we call the forty years in the wilderness God's design ! He sets aside the idea by that one significant word, "provocation," that is what He calls it, "the provoking," "the day of temptation in the wilderness, when your fathers tempted me, proved me, and saw my works forty years. Wherefore, I was grieved with that generation, and said, They do alway err in their. heart ; and they have not known my ways. So I sware in my wrath," — less than eighteen months after their redemption from Egypt the Eternal God 'sware in His wrath that they should not enter into His rest,' and they did not! Their carcases fell in the wilderness. Why, for years, I thought I must reproduce in my individual experience, that of the children of Israel; that I was bound to have ups and downs, patches of sand, green oases ; a time of sterility and a time of prayerfullness ; the hour of cold and the hour of heat. Oh ! it is high time that we search in the records of God's word and see whether indeed "these things be so."

Now, listen: "Take heed, brethren, lest there be in any of you an evil heart of unbelief, in departing from the living God." Many Christians speak about their hearts as still being "deceitful above all things, and desperately wicked." I cannot join them. What! shall God give me a new heart and a right spirit, yea, a new life in Christ, and shall I have a vision of my soul as filled with the corrupt evil thing that has passed away? No, brethren, it is not true. As well might you say that the new life God has given you is a poor, dwarfed, diseased thing. I pray you, do not thus dishonor Him. Many Christians think of their spiritual life as of a diseased thing, which, after years and years, is, by a sort of purging process, to be purified. It is not so, — liable to wander, we may be, — not prone.

Shall I insult my Lord by saying that after getting possession of the new heart, — after the stony heart is taken away, — I still have a heart that cannot believe Him, that is always departing from Him? Listen, brethren: In the day of our conversion we had entrance into the holiest of all, by the blood of Jesus: but by all the solemn testimony of that word you and I have never had liberty to go out again forever. If we do, it is a voluntary act — a deliberate sin. Do not talk of approaching unto God, — "Ye *are* come," says the Apostle, "to the Father." I beg of you go no more away forever.

And now, just one or two other verses, and I
have done. "But exhort one another daily, while
it is called to-day,"—is not that beautiful, "to-day."
Again, "Lest any of you be hardened through the
deceitfulness of sin. For we are made partakers
of Christ, if we hold the beginning of our confidence steadfast unto the end." There is the life of
faith, you see,—not a principle in operation and
then laid aside,—but kept in continual operation,
always, always in use. Then look at this: "While
it is said, 'to-day.'" Oh! I press that "to-day"
upon you, as if God could not bear this night of
unbelief to set in, with its dense darkness. "To-
day, if ye will hear His voice, harden not your
hearts, as in the provocation. For some, when
they had heard, did provoke: howbeit not all that
came out of Egypt by Moses. But with whom was
He grieved forty years? Was it not with them
that had sinned, whose carcases fell in the wilderness? And to whom sware He that they should
not enter into His rest, but to them that believed
not? So we see that they could not enter in,
because of unbelief." Let me remind every child
of God here of this solemn thought— God cannot
believe for you,—belief must be your own act. I
would that you might grasp the idea of Paul in the
Acts: "In Him we live, and move, and have our
being." Not physically, only, but in the length,
breadth, depth and height of our spiritual life.
And now see the first verse of the fourth chapter
of Hebrews: "Let us therefore fear, lest, a promise
being left us of entering into His rest, any of you

should seem to come short of it. For unto us was
the gospel preached, as well as unto them; but the
word preached did not profit them, not being mixed
with faith in them that heard it. For we which
have believed, do enter into rest." Bless God for
the rest of faith! It is no chimera, no empty
dream, — it is the calm rest of the soul upon the
Eternal Lord, — it is the very antithesis of pride,
it cannot live in the atmosphere of presumption.
Mark what I say, — all boasting is excluded. By
what? The law of works? Nay, but by the law
of faith.

Brethren, it was this horrid sin of unbelief that
broke off the Jews from their own olive tree.
"Thou standest by faith." Oh, God, keep us from
unbelief! Child of God, never for a moment har-
bor the thought that God is absent from thee.
Hath He not said, "I will never leave thee, I will
never forsake thee." Remember that wonderful
expression in second Corinthians, ninth chapter,
eleventh verse, "Being enriched in *everything*, to
all bountifulness, which causeth through us thanksgiving to God." That is faith's language, — not
"going to be enriched," but "being enriched." It
is this unbelief which shuts God entirely out of
great departments of our being, making a hundred
weight of trouble become a ton; building prospec-
tive sorrows, nine-tenths of which never come to
pass at all. And shall it always be thus? Are we
never to form the holy habit of faith in God? This
phrase, "holy habit," was a new thought to me,
until presented to me lately by a brother in Eng-

land, and I then saw that by it the coming of
unbelief to the front was prevented. I pray you
cultivate this habit of faith. Vitiate not God's
promises, --stagger not at seeming impossibilities.
I bless God for that word used of Abraham, "He
staggered not." There was enough to have seem-
ingly excused it in him ; but God had promised,
and that was enough. 'Through faith they sub-
dued kingdoms, wrought righteousness, stopped the
mouths of lions, quenched the violence of fire ; out
of weakness were made strong, waxed valiant in
fight, turned to flight the armies of aliens.' The
same principle ; and, again I remind you, these two
opposite principles cannot dominate at the same
time. No, no, no !

Let me leave with you one illustration of the
power of this. You will find it at the beginning
of the sixth chapter of the Second Corinthians.
"We then, as workers together with God, beseech
you, that ye receive not the grace of God in vain ;
for He saith, I have heard thee in a time accepted,
and in the day of salvation have I succored thee :
behold, now is the accepted time ; behold, now is
the day of salvation." The reference here is to the
exalted Christ, out of whose fullness the entire
Church has received, not according to our moral
fitness, but according to His grace. Now listen :
" Giving no offence in anything, that the ministry
be not blamed." This is what the life of faith says,
and I feel disposed to ask,—Tell me, Paul, we are
fellow-servants in the kingdom of our Lord ; do
you mean, that in your life, so full of anxiety and

trial, and what we call emergency, is this your daily rule?

He speaks again in the fourth verse, "But in all things approving ourselves as the ministers of God." Do you mean that? Am I to accept this double expression of yours? Yes, replies the Apostle: "in afflictions, in necessities, in distresses, in stripes, in imprisonments, in tumults, in labors, in watchings, in fastings." Why, do you mean, that in the midst of these circumstances, this mass of trying ordeals,—ten of them mentioned,—and each one seeming to me enough to break down the strongest spirit, you affirm that you acquit yourself without blame? Oh! let me know how it is done. Here, the majority of us are beaten back by circumstances; do show us the secret of it!

In the next two verses, he takes us as it were into the very engine room. Being in Aberdeen some time since, I went into the granite works, and saw hundreds of belts going in every direction, and the saws working away at the granite. I asked how long it would take to cut through one particular block, and was told, four months of constant sawing. "Where is your power?" said I. He took me into a place called the engine-house, and there I saw the power which set all the saws in motion, and kept them so. And that is where Paul takes us:— "By pureness, by knowledge, by long suffering, by kindness, by the Holy Ghost." Oh! yes. I begin to see that great vital forces are at your command. "By love unfeigned, by the word of truth, by the power of God, by the armor of righteousness on

the right hand and on the left." Oh! I wonder no
longer. If that is the capital with which you work,
your success does not astonish me.

If one of your capitalists should desire to send a
friend to open a branch business for him in a neighboring city, and just as he was starting, should say
to him : " Of course you understand you are to
furnish all the capital;" do you suppose he would
undertake it ? Brethren and sisters, we profess to
be alive unto God, living for His glory, working in
His employ ; and I believe that the results of our
lives are so meagre because, instead of working
with His capital, we are trying to work with our
own ; and so Paul adds, "by honor and dishonor."
What, don't you care whether people honor or dishonor you ? " Not the least," says he ; "just as
soon serve the Master one way as another ;" "by
evil report and good report ;" " as deceivers " —
only put the other side — "and yet true;" "as
unknown" to man, "and yet well known," to God ;
"as dying," to self, sin, and the world, "and behold
we live," or Christ lives in us ; " as sorrowful, yet
alway rejoicing ; as poor, yet making many rich ;
as having nothing, and yet possessing all things."

Oh! friends, it is truly sublime to get into the
genius of the life of faith. I have sometimes
likened Paul to a miller, and one comes up with a
sack of honor on his back. " Put it in," says Paul,
and grinds away. Another comes with a sack of
dishonor. " Strange brand," says Paul, " but put it
in." Now comes one with a sack of evil report.
" What field in Corinth does that come from," says

Paul, "but turn it in." All goes into his mill, and he works away ; for you see he is not trading on his own resources ; he has learned to live the life of faith on the Son of God. " O ye Corinthians," he exclaims, "our mouth is open unto you, our heart is enlarged ; now for a recompense in the same, be ye also enlarged." Put out this dastardly sin ; down with it at any cost ; and say, on your knees before God, " By all that I, as a child of faith, have known of Thy gracious power, O Son of God, I beseech Thee to cast out the horrid power of this demon sin of my life." AMEN.

THE

POWER OF FAITH.

ROMANS IV. 20.

HE STAGGERED NOT AT THE PROMISE OF GOD THROUGH UN-
BELIEF; BUT WAS STRONG IN FAITH, GIVING GLORY TO
GOD.

HAVING spoken on the sin of unbelief, I wish
to call your attention to the subject of faith.
Our Christian life is a life of faith upon the
Son of God. If we continuously exercise faith, we
shall "win along the whole line" of our life. If we
are weak in faith, we must to that extent fail; if we
are strong in faith, there cannot be failure. I desire
now your very thoughtful attention, and I shall be
glad if those that have their Bibles will turn with
me to one very striking example you will find in
the book of Numbers, of how faith held its position
in the midst of very great difficulties. You know
the common idea is, that if our circumstances were
different, faith would be easier of exercise;—we
forget that faith is superior to circumstances.

That is the truth, however, — faith is superior to circumstances.

Now, take such a thought as this. Has it ever struck you that the Lord Jesus, though He was Lord of all — and there can be no doubt it will not be irreverent of me to say it — if He had thought when He lived in Judea and carried on His public ministry, that a large estate, a well furnished house and plenty of money would have helped Him, He would surely have availed Himself of them ? And yet the remarkable fact is before us, that He voluntarily chose a condition of self-abnegation and poverty on purpose to teach us that our life does not consist in the abundance of the things that we possess. It is a thought worthy of our very deepest consideration, that the Lord of all was content to be in this position of voluntary poverty. And now to our illustration.

I am going to take the case of Caleb. Will you look at the thirteenth chapter of the book of Numbers. You will find that Caleb was one of the heads of the tribes who were sent by Moses to spy out the land. We will read at the twenty-fifth verse : " And they returned from searching of the land after forty days. And they went and came to Moses, and to Aaron, and to all the congregation of the children of Israel, * * * And they told him, and said, We came unto the land whither thou sentest us, and surely it floweth with milk and honey ; and this is the fruit of it. Nevertheless the people be strong that dwell in the land, and the cities are walled, and very great: and moreover

3

we saw the children of Anak there. * * * And
Caleb stilled the people before Moses, and said "—
Mark the utterances of the man of faith, — I have
noticed, again and again, how faith not only holds
its own but infuses its courage among others.

It was just so with David when, before the fight
with Goliath, the very first words he uttered before
King Saul, after he had volunteered to fight, were:
"Let no man's heart fail because of him."

Now just look at a stripling youth like David,
sending a mighty tide of courage right out through
all the hosts of Israel. Then Caleb, just in the
same spirit, "stilled the people before Moses,
and said, Let us go up at once." That is what
faith always says. If you are going to dilly-dally
with it, you will find yourselves in difficulty. "Let
us go up at once, and possess it; for we are well
able to overcome it. But the men that went up
with him said, We be not able to go up against the
people; for they are stronger than we." That is
what unbelief always says. "And they brought
up an evil report of the land * * * saying, The
land, through which we have gone to search it, is a
land that eateth up the inhabitants thereof; and all
the people that we saw in it are men of great
stature."

Now just a thought about that. If you will look
at the twenty-second verse you will see that the
very place where they saw the men of great stature
was Hebron. "And they ascended by the south,
and came unto Hebron; where Ahiman, Sheshai,
and Talmai, the children of Anak, were." Now

observe, Caleb was a man whose business it was to
go and search for Hebron, and though, so far as
the history informs us, the sons of Anak were not
met with except in Hebron, and though Caleb saw
what the others did not see, yet he looked the difficulty in the face, and he said, 'Despite the sons
of Anak we are going to overcome.' Now mark
that, — it is an important point, and the bearing
of it upon the after part of my address will be
seen. "And there we saw the giants, the sons of
Anak, which come of the giants : and we were in
our own sight as grasshoppers, and so we were
in their sight." As I have already pointed out
to you, that is one of the most cowardly expressions that unbelief ever could have affirmed.
We have no objection to their own little estimation
of themselves, but to get this from the enemies'
side, is too bad. However, unbelief is quite able
to do that. "And the whole congregation said
unto them," — I am reading this verse to show
how unbelief prevails, and yet how faith holds its
own in the midst of universal failure, — " And the
whole congregation said unto them, Would God
that we had died in the land of Egypt! or would
God we had died in this wilderness! And wherefore hath the Lord brought us unto this land, to
fall by the sword, that our wives and our children
should be a prey? were it not better for us to
return into Egypt?"

Now just think of a redeemed believer saying
this. They had only a little time before stood on
the banks of the Red Sea and seen their enemies

sink beneath the mighty waves like stones, or "like
lead," as Miriam puts it. And then they said,
"Would God that we had died in this wilderness!
And wherefore hath the Lord brought us unto this
land, to fall by the sword,"—isn't it terrible to tell
God to His face that He has brought them into
the land, to fall by the sword?—that our wives
and our children should be a prey? were it not
better for us to return into Egypt? And they said
one to another, Let us make a captain, and let us
return into Egypt. Then Moses and Aaron fell on
their faces before all the assembly of the congregation of the children of Israel. And Joshua the
son of Nun, and Caleb the son of Jephunneh, which
were of them that searched the land, rent their
clothes : And they spake unto all the company of
the children of Israel, saying, The land, which we
passed through to search it, is an exceeding good
land."

Right in the ferment of this opposition does
God's faithful servant speak out : "If the Lord
delight in us, then He will bring us into this land,
and give it us; a land which floweth with milk
and honey. Only rebel not ye against the Lord,
neither fear ye the people of the land." Oh! the
beautiful combination there! Look at it,—no
rebellion,—God. No controversy with us,—loyal
hearts. I say that, because you know the danger
to which so many of God's people expose themselves is, that while they are prepared to give up
thirty-eight things, they will stick to the other two.
Now, dear friends, I want to say this to you,—it is

the things you do not give up, that God must have
contention with you about. I will suppose that
there is a husband living in some semi-detached
villa outside of the suburbs of your city, and that
in the next house there lives a very fashionable
woman, but still a woman of very questionable
character. There is not a husband here that would
like his wife to have anything to say to her. But
suppose your wife would say: " I know you have a
very strong feeling about this, and I will not visit
her except five minutes a week." Well, your contention with her would be about that five minutes.
And it is so with the things God does not want
you to have. You must give up the whole of
them, so as to have a conscience devoid of sin.
"Only rebel not ye against the Lord, neither fear
ye the people of the land ; for they are bread for
us." Oh! that is simply magnificent. At the close
of the last chapter they were looking back, completely overcome, but this man says: ' They are
bread for us; I am going to feed on them day
after day,' for ' Their defence is departed from
them, and the Lord is with us: fear them not.
But all the congregation bade stone them with
stones." Just look at what unbelief can do. It
can actually come with its pile of stones and call
on its votaries to slay outright the man of faith.

Well, how now ? Did these men give up their
confidence? Just listen: "And the glory of the
Lord appeared in the tabernacle of the congregation before all the children of Israel." God had
come to the defence of His children. What a

beautiful harmony there is between the fourth of
Romans, where it says, "strong in faith, giving
glory to God," and the glory of God coming to the
defence of faith.

And now, dear brethren, I want to show you the
sequel of this. You must pardon my introduction
trenching somewhat on my address the other afternoon, but I had a purpose in doing it, and that
purpose I now proceed to show you. Let us
turn to the fourteenth chapter of the book of
Joshua. I told you how, in consequence of their
rejection of the land of promise, God sware in
His wrath that this generation of the children
of Israel should not enter into His rest. They
never did, — every man of them died out, and
their bones bleached in the wilderness, until there
was not a man of them left save Caleb and Joshua.
Between the chapter to which I call your attention and our other reading, you must place
an interval of forty-five years. Now observe these
words, — the sixth verse. The children of Israel
are in the land, — Joshua has led them on unto
great conquests: "Then the children of Judah
came unto Joshua in Gilgal: and Caleb the son
of Jephunneh the Kenezite, said unto him, Thou
knowest the thing that the Lord said unto Moses
the man of God concerning me and thee in Kadesh-
barnea. Forty years old was I when Moses the
servant of the Lord sent me from Kadesh-barnea
to espy out the land ; and I brought him word
again as it was in mine heart. Nevertheless my
brethren that went up with me made the heart of

the people melt: but I wholly followed the Lord
my God. And Moses sware on that day, saying,
Surely the land whereon thy feet have trodden
shall be thine inheritance, and thy children's forever, because thou hast wholly followed the Lord
my God."

Mark the descent here, — the children of faith,
not the children of the Kenezites, — 'Thy children's forever, because thou hast wholly followed
the Lord my God. And now, behold, the Lord hath
kept me alive.' See how that is put. He does
not say natural force has kept me alive, you see, —
he says: 'God hath kept me alive.' Why, it is
God's great business to keep faith alive. Certainly
it is. He hath kept me alive "these forty and five
years, even since the Lord spake this word unto
Moses." And then observe, when the children of
Israel wandered in the wilderness: "And now,
behold, the Lord hath kept me alive, as He said,
these forty and five years, even since the Lord
spake this word unto Moses, while the children of
Israel wandered in the wilderness: and now, lo, I
am this day fourscore and five years old."

Grand old man! Outliving the generation of
unbelievers! Ah! it is faith's genius to do this.
Faith will always see unbelief dying out, — certainly
she must. Faith always survives the generation of
unbelievers, according to a law that knows no
repeal. And listen: "As yet I am as strong this
day as I was in the day that Moses sent me: as
my strength was then, even so is my strength now,
for war." I like that, — there is a symbol of the

higher life. You are not allowed to fall into indolence, — no indeed, — " for war." See the old man : " For war, both to go out, and to come in."

Brethren and sisters, I have a very solemn thought for you, and let me be careful. It may be that I am addressing some Christian sister or brother who has inherited a weakly physical frame. I need scarcely say, to such a one my remarks do not refer. But I say this, — if I am addressing a Christian youth or maiden here this morning, — my sister, my brother, listen. Know that Jesus Christ hath bought thy body : yield it to Him, and He will be the great Conservator of the forces of thy being and He will keep thy strength. Mind what I say, — for lack of this whole-hearted faith in the Lord, it is written in the First Epistle to the Corinthians : " For this cause many are weak and sickly among you," and some God has judged with death, — " some sleep." You do not belong to yourselves.

How many a Christian man I have known in the old country drop off, as it is called, in the world! They have been in the same Bible class with me. They have been in the same class in the Sunday school. They have prospered, as the world calls it, and they have got into certain companionships and fellowships of the world, and I suppose that the dignity of the gospel of Christ has not been enough for some of them, and so we have missed them, and they have lost their vital force as Christians in the luxuriance of their richly furnished houses ; and Christian sisters have lazily lounged upon their cushions, and wasted the precious hours in bed, when their circumstances seemed to say, you may take it easy. And I have seen them lose their physical figure, and become *nil* in the Church, and I believe for neither more nor less than that they had just given themselves up to an unholy self-pleasing instead of a devoted love of Christ.

The Master said, and He means it: "I am come that ye might have life, and that ye might have it more abundantly." But, "If any man will come after me, let him deny himself and take up his cross and follow me." Oh! brethren, these are searching words. Again I say it, Christian sister, if you want to retain the strength which you have now, if you want to be a hale mother in Israel, blessing, perhaps, the second and third generations, see to it that you follow God ; and perchance like good Gideon, or good old Caleb, you will say, 'I am this day fourscore and five years old, and yet I am as strong this day as I was in the day when the Lord spake unto me.' And now listen: "Now, therefore, give me this mountain, whereof the Lord spake in that day; for thou heardest in that day how the Anakim were there, and that the cities were great and fenced ; *if so be the Lord will be*," I am sorry that I have read that "will be," but you see it has been suggested by the translators. "Will be" is not in the original, — very important that fact. It is not "will be," — there is no idea of "will be" with the faithful. *It is* so. Then look: "I shall be able to drive them out, as the Lord said." "I shall be able," — no doubt about that.

"And Joshua blessed him, and gave unto Caleb the son of Jephunneh Hebron for an inheritance."

Now some people charge us with holding the so called doctrine of perfection. I trust I need scarcely say, that it is not true. I confess I never felt so deep a need of the precious blood of Christ. I do feel that sin is so interwoven with the very woof and warp of our being that I should deprecate, more than words can tell, any such feeling as that I did not need the precious blood. And you know that if I held, or any one else held, the idea of perfection, such a thought as that I have been expressing could not be held at the same time. But I do say this, that it is of the highest moment to us that like good old Caleb, we should not misunderstand. In his case he comes and he expects to get the inheritance that God had promised.

And what are we to expect, as we, God's children, walk through the world? Are we to be forgotten and trodden down by our enemies? Is sin to have dominion over us? Surely not. Here this grand old man expelled his enemies. It is not said that he slew them, for he did not do that, and I want you to note the distinction. It is our bounden duty, as it is our highest privilege, to expel our enemies, — not slay them. If you will carefully search this subject out for yourselves, I think you will find, by every fair inference,—indeed, to my mind it is conclusive, — that Joshua slew these expelled enemies. Joshua slew them,—Caleb expelled them.

It is your duty and mine to cleanse ourselves from all filthiness, so that we shall be vessels fit for the Master's use ; but let us never forget that while it is ours to expel, it is our Joshua's to put to death. " Hebron therefore became the inheritance of Caleb the son of Jephunneh the Kenezite unto this day ; because that he wholly followed the Lord God of Israel." Now, to what have I brought you? Do you know the meaning of the word Hebron? It means "friendship," "fellowship." That is the inheritance of a heart fully given up to God. And brethren, we are in a better position than Caleb was in this respect ; for you see Caleb was kept out of his possession for forty-five years by the disobedience of the people that surrounded him. Thank God the unbelief of others need not keep us out of our inheritance now. And again let me repeat that ; it is of the highest moment. I say, that in consequence of Caleb's position, he was kept out of his earthly inheritance forty-five years by the surrounding unbelief. God preserved him and kept him alive ; but we have this advantage, that the unbelief common in our day need not keep us out of our inheritance one single hour.

"Hebron." Oh! what a word that is, "friendship," "fellowship," union with a living God and His heritage! If I were asked to give the New Testament equivalent of this, I would remind you of the words of the beloved disciple :—" Our fellowship is with the Father, and with His Son Jesus Christ." "And the name of Hebron before was Kirjath-arba ; which Arba was a great man among the Anakim. And the land had rest from war."

I want to take you a little further, to show you Caleb in his possession. Will you turn now to the first chapter of the book of Judges. It is astonishing how the Bible is its own expositor. May I just say to my brethren the ministers here, that we do great violence to the Bible by not making it its own exponent. I find one of the most profitable methods of study of the Word of God is to do this, supposing a word strikes me— you know very often a subject is contained in just a word :—one of Mr. Moody's most profitable Bible exercises is an address that he gives on " heaven," and he takes the Concordance, and carefully deals with the passages in which the word occurs, and there is a wonderful train of connection. And so of any subject. But this is just an illustration in passing.

In the first chapter of Judges, twelfth and thirteenth verses, you read this : "And Caleb said, He that smiteth Kirjath-sepher, and taketh it, to him will I give Achsah my daughter to wife. And Othniel the son of Kenaz, Caleb's younger brother, took it : and he gave him Achsah his daughter to wife." How remarkable it is that faith has not only its own personal, individual strength, but that it has also a relative blessing to bestow. I have no doubt that this young man, this nephew of Caleb's, had had his eye upon his uncle, knew the force of his uncle's character, and so says young Othniel I'll just go and attack that stronghold, that Kirjath-sepher." "I will go," and he pledges his word; he has partaken of his uncle's courage.

You know some one has said, "One man of faith will shake the country for ten miles round;" and there is no mistake about it. I will venture to say that God does not want money, but men and women. Oh let us say to-day, we are ready for the Master's use. I have sometimes given an illustration of this kind in the old country. I dare say that some of the good housewives here know what it is to have in the table drawer in the kitchen a number of knives; and I should not be in the least surprised if there was a friendship between you and one of those knives. You want a piece of bread quickly cut, and though that knife is not as new as some of its bright fellows, it has a keen edge on it, and you will pass by all the other knives and take it. And why? Because there is a keen edge on it. So if you will go and run your keen edge of character on the world, sawing it backward and forward all your life, do you think God will blunt you? He will not. Tell me the measure of a man's devotion, the measure of a man's surrender to God, and I will tell you the limit of his powers.

I am not now touching the question of gift, but of fitness for the service of the Master. Oh! that you and I may just realize how important this is! how it is everything to us—"meet for the Master's use." "And it came to pass, when she came to him," that is, after the marriage, "that she moved him to ask of her father a field: and she lighted

3*

from off her ass; and Caleb said unto her, What
wilt thou? And she said unto him, Give me a
blessing." Ah! dear child, she has not known her
father for years for naught. She knows that there
is power to impart in the hands of a man of faith,
and availing herself of her relationship and her
father's possessions, she says, "For thou hast given
me a south land; give me also springs of water."
He had given his daughter a south land, sunny and
pleasant. I am afraid that some Christians go
and get planted under a north-east wall where the
winds blow. They want transplanting. They want
to be where they can sing, "The winter is over
and gone; the time of the singing of birds is come;
and the voice of the turtle is heard in our land."

In the "south land." Yes, sunny and pleasant.
Blessed, blessed thought. "Give me also springs of
water. And Caleb gave her the upper springs and
the nether springs." Oh! what a beautiful finish
is this. "The upper springs" with their measure-
less fullness! But mark you, he gave her "the
upper springs and the nether." Brethren, that is
our position with God. We are receiving and we
are pouring out that we have received amongst our
fellow men. If I were to go into one of your houses,
and should see there a cistern remarkably full of
water, and if I knew that that cistern was in connection with your water works, and that there was
no ball cock there, I should come to this conclusion,
that the water works were just on a level with the
top of your cistern. But if I saw that cistern running over, I should come to the conclusion that it

was in connection with a water supply perhaps up
in the mountain a few miles back there; and that it
was running over because of the height of that
water supply.

Now, I say to every Christian here to-day, that
if you do not run over, it is a great shame. And
I press this upon you, because it is not simply
fullness that we want. If your heart is full of
grace this afternoon, there is not much room for
the world; but though you be filled from the fountain, it is not enough, for I am persuaded it is the
overflow that blesses others. I know that it is
easier to preach when I am overflowing in this
way, when, as the Psalmist puts it in that forty-fifth
Psalm, "My heart is inditing," or as the marginal
reading is, "bubbling up." When the living springs
are just coming up like that, it is easy to speak.

When I was in Chesterfield, England, I went
to visit the house of one whose name is one of
very great fame to most of us here,—the great
George Stephenson, who you know did so much to
introduce railways among us in England. There
was his great house. I was very sorry to see it,
because it was in chancery, and very few things
that get into chancery ever get out of it again. As
I went through the suites of rooms, I saw the one
in which he died. We got in at one of the windows
at first. The house was so desolate,—scarcely a
fly; a few spiders crawling about the wall seemed
to be the only living tenants of the place. We
went out into the back yard and our guide came to
us there, and said: "Gentlemen, be careful; there's

a well here. Some logs of wood have been put across it, but you must be careful." I approached it, and looked down through the logs, and the sunlight was shining down, and do you know, that water was the only living thing in that empty scene! There, a hundred feet deep at the least, could be seen the beautiful stream playing at the bottom and forcing the water up, and as I looked at it, I thought, Oh! may the blessing of God give me to know something of the everlasting springs, that when weakness comes there may be no failure.

In Wales, a few years ago, one hot July day, a gentleman was passing through—one of our English tourists — and as he was going along the hot and dusty road, a little girl met him, carrying an earthen pitcher full of spring water on her head. He said to her: "My child, will you give me a draught of water?" and she lifted the jug from her head, and he drank from it, and it was so cold, and pure and beautiful, that he asked, "Where do you get that beautiful water from?" and she said to him, "Do you see up yonder? there's a spring coming through the hedge." "Yes; and does that spring ever dry up?" The little girl said, "Yes, in the summer it dries up." "And what do you do then?" he asked her. "Do you see a path up the hill to another spring?" she said. "Well, does it ever dry up?" he inquired. "Yes," she said, "two or three summers ago it dried up." "And what do you do then?" the gentleman asked. "We go up to the spring at the top." "And does it never dry up?" "Oh, no," she said, "it never dries up, away up there."

Brethren, I have led you to the fountain that never dries up. Hebron never dries up. Hebron! Oh! the inheritance! I pray you enter upon it. I pray you take up your abode upon it. If unbelief has kept you out of it; if love of sin has kept you from it; if neglect of the study of this book has kept you from this priceless property—and many a Christian is in this condition—know that you have this immense estate left you. If knowing this you do not enter upon it, you are as foolish as if the document which gave you legal right to an earthly estate had been put away in the dusty office of some solicitor in your city, and though you could prove your legal right to it, you were still living in the six-roomed house in that street where you had been living for the last twenty years. That is the way with many Christians; they are just living as though they had the title deed and nothing more.

Oh! that we may hear the Master saying to us to-day, "Freely ye have received; freely give." I do not know what you would think if I had lived in England and invited you to come and visit me, and you found me living in the lodge at the gate. I imagine I see you in one of our English wagonettes. You see my well known figure emerging from the lodge beyond the little iron gates, and I say, "I'm so happy to see you, pray walk inside;" and you hesitate, and another, and another, until one says, "We are a little diffident about it; it is true we came out to see you, but you are not living at the lodge?" "Oh! yes." "But there's a magnificent mansion up there behind those trees." "Well, the fact is, I have never been to see it." "But there's a magnificent view from those hills up there, and the estate I believe covers a very great number of acres." "But the fact is, ever since I have been here I have resided at the lodge, and have never gone to look at the estate."

Some of you will say, that I would not do that, and I say you are right. But how many of you are living at the lodge to-day? You have just come inside, and set foot in the path of Jesus. A little of the light of heaven has shone upon you, but you have lived in the lodge. God help you to leave it, to say to-day, "I will change the lodge for the mansion, penury for plenty, spiritual poverty for spiritual wealth." For, blessed be God, it is written, 'All spiritual blessings are ours in heavenly places in Christ'—our possession, our right. "Lo, I am with you alway, even unto the end." Reckon yourselves dead unto sin and dead to the world, but alive unto God with your portion in heaven.

Brethren, mark my closing words. You and I are wont to communicate with our friends, and we have been accustomed to date our letters from our residences ; bear with me in saying it, (and I would impress the reality upon your hearts,) you have just as much reason to write "heaven" there if you are partakers of that life. Oh! Great Father, help us not only to look at the truth, and see it by intellectual perception, but may it become a force, a life, a home, that shall be seen by our fellow men to Thy glory. AMEN.

CHRISTIAN RESPONSIBILITY.

II CORINTHIANS v. 10.

FOR WE MUST ALL APPEAR BEFORE THE JUDGMENT SEAT OF
CHRIST; THAT EVERY ONE MAY RECEIVE THE THINGS DONE
IN HIS BODY, ACCORDING TO THAT HE HATH DONE, WHETHER
IT BE GOOD OR BAD.

THESE words, beloved friends, do not represent the condemnation that the ungodly will realize at the judgment of the great white throne. They represent the judgment by the Lord Jesus Christ upon His servants at His coming. I beg of you remember that. They have no reference to the unconverted at all. They belong to God's people, and to them alone. "We must all appear," every one of us. As the servants of Jesus Christ we must be manifested at the judgment seat of Christ, and we shall receive for the things that we have done in the body according to that we have done, "whether it be good or bad." How manifestly important this thought! See where its rise is. In the very hour in which your responsibility

to God as a sinner ceases through faith in Jesus
Christ, in that hour your responsibility as His child
begins. You venture into a new position. Let
me show you by a very simple illustration. Here
are two kingdoms — one the kingdom of darkness,
the other the kingdom of light, — and the very hour
you are converted you are translated, — taken from
the one kingdom and placed in the other kingdom.
You have left that kingdom forever. You have
come into the kingdom of light and life. You have
come forth from the kingdom of Satan and come
under the sceptre of the Prince of Peace, the
Lord Jesus Christ ; and as there was condemnation
there, there is justification here. I beg of you to
give local identity to the thought, for your position
is as much changed as though you had been living
in the desert of Siberia, and had been brought
to the sweet tropical climate of Ceylon. Do not
forget that, — it is of the highest moment. If you
"play fast and loose," — sometimes in this country
and sometimes in that, — you will never know what
it is to be established in peace.

When we come to stand before the Lord our
Prince, we shall find that heaven is not a medley ;
heaven is not a heterogeneous assembly, all ushered
in through an open door to take one place and one
position. As you leave off here, you will begin
there. One once said to Wesley concerning Whitefield, — you know that the controversy between
Arminians and Calvinists, as they were called in
those days, waxed very hot, and in the heat of the
bad feeling it was not uncommon to hear doubts

expressed by the partisans of Whitefield as to whether Mr. Wesley would be saved, and by the partisans of Wesley as to whether Mr. Whitefield would be saved, — one said to Mr. Wesley : " Do you think we shall see Whitefield in heaven ?" and when thus appealed to, Mr. Wesley said : " No, I do not think we shall, for he will be so near the throne and we so far away, that we shall not get a glimpse of him."

Ah ! sirs, I want you to remember this, that the Lord God beseeches us as Christians not to lose the full reward. I hear men say sometimes : " I have been converted ten years." If so, brother, you ought to be a long way on, — your views of the Divine light should be very large. The grasp of the truth upon you should be wonderful by this time. Ten years living upon Christ ! Ten years of His development ! Ten years of His grace in operation in your soul ! Oh ! what a beautiful character yours should be. I press these thoughts upon you because, when I turn to the First Epistle to the Corinthians, and read such words as these in the third chapter, where Paul is speaking to those who are laboring together with God : " For we are laborers together with God : ye are God's husbandry, ye are God's building. According to the grace of God which is given unto me, as a wise masterbuilder, I have laid the foundation, and another buildeth thereon. But let every man take heed how he buildeth thereupon. For other foundation can no man lay than that is laid, which is Jesus Christ. Now if any man build upon this foundation gold, silver, precious stones, wood, hay, stubble ;"—look at the contrast,—the gold, the silver, the precious stones, — these are the acceptable things—these are the things that will stand the fire.

I dare say some of you remember that terrible accident on the North Western Railway, the Irish mail, when a certain English nobleman and his wife were burned to ashes, with eighteen others, when those terrible petroleum casks took fire. It is said that in the carriage where the nobleman and his wife were, they were completely burned to ashes, but by a careful search after the fire, some jewels were found that the lady had purchased in London, and was taking with her to her home in Ireland. And mark what I say to you. If you build upon that one foundation, all your life after conversion, "Whether ye eat or drink, or whatsoever ye do, do all to the glory of God."

A dear girl in our Sunday School greatly pleased me some time ago. She left Notting Hill and went to her first situation, and, some time afterwards, writing to one of her Sunday School teachers, she said : "I miss the services of the Tabernacle very much, but there is one thing which helps me greatly. Our pastor told me one Sunday that everything we did, we might do for Jesus Christ ·" and she said — it made me smile but was nevertheless forcible—"When I clean master's boots, I think if I were doing them for Jesus, wouldn't I make them shine ?" I tell you, when we just grasp the reality of that dear child's one thought, and communicate it to the whole of our character, our life will become simply beautiful. You cannot be unkind for Christ's sake, you cannot be selfish for Christ's sake, you cannot speak evil of your fellow Christians for Christ's sake, you cannot do wrong for Christ's sake. No man would sit down and drink a bottle of wine for Christ's sake, or pamper appetite for Christ's sake. Take heed how you build thereupon, for mark, "Every man's work shall be made manifest : for the day shall declare it," the very day of which my text speaks to you, "because it shall be revealed by fire ; and the fire shall try every man's work of what sort it is. If any man's work abide which he hath built thereupon, he shall receive a reward ; if any man's work shall be burned he shall suffer loss."

Oh ! but brethren, what does this mean ? "But himself shall be saved ; yet though as by fire." His works burned up, himself saved ; all the works burned up, himself saved! This is one sad extreme. This is the result to the unfaithful child of God. This comes of the non-recognition of our responsibility to God as His child ; for again I remind you, the very hour when your responsibility to God as a sinner ceases, your responsibility as God's child begins. Oh! important thought! Dear friends, read it; get it graven upon your hearts : — "My responsibility as God's child begins in the very hour that I enter His family."

And now, I direct your thoughts to the 'crowns' of Scripture, as elucidating my text. You have read, have you not, of the "crown of life"? Now,

I venture to say to you, that the crown of life is the common property of all the saved. It is the equivalent of that word at the close of the third chapter of John, "He that believeth on the Son hath everlasting life;" and there are none of the saved that have not this crown. But I hear Paul say, "I have fought a good fight, I have finished my course, I have kept the faith : henceforth there is laid up for me a crown of righteousness." Mark you, not the "crown of life," the "crown of righteousness which the Lord the righteous Judge" — do you see that ? —"the Lord, the righteous Judge, shall give me in that day." Now, what is that crown of righteousness ? I believe that it is on our part the faithful recognition of our service, of our sonship, so that we strive lawfully, that we work perseveringly, that we do not make a child's play of our discipleship. To us it is a reality in that we are redeemed. We recognize that we are bought with a price, and that therefore we ought to "glorify God in our bodies and in our spirits which are His." And so after a careful, painstaking and faithful service, the Master crowns us with the crown of righteousness. It is not a crown as though He were indebted to us, but it is grace's crown. Jesus loves to put — shall I say laurel?—about the brows that are His, and we are warned not to lose a "full reward." Therefore, I will say to you, be not content with simply being saved, but let your life be the good fight for the crown of righteousness.

I remember being very much struck with a testimony that I heard of one of our London barristers,

who was a young man, yet a Christian. He had
prospered in his profession. He mingled a good
deal with our professional London men, and the
effect of dinner parties and that sort of thing was
hurtful to his spiritual life. He had a very remarkable dream. He dreamed that he was gone from
the world. His spirit was conducted by angelic
ministers with haste away from this world, and he
entered the hall of an immense and splendid mansion. He said, no words could tell the splendor of
the scene that he gazed upon. As he stood looking
upon it, the angels who had conducted him thither
entered into conversation one with another, and he
overheard this, " Oh!" said one of the angels, "this
was to have been his house ; it was designed for
him ; it was the ' mansion prepared ' and all furnished, but early in his life he forsook the devoted
service of Christ, and went back in heart into the
spirit of the world, and it is not adapted for him
now. We must take him away." And as the
angels were in the act of conducting him away
from this scene of splendor to some lower one, the
violence of his emotion awoke him suddenly.

Ah ! but there is truth in the man's dream.
There are many and many who will have in contrast to what they might have, very little, because
they fail to recognize the grandeur of the service
of Christ. I repeat it, as that book is true, as you
and I leave off here, we shall begin in the world to
come.

In the First Epistle of Peter and in the fifth
chapter you will find a crown spoken of, which is

4

neither the crown of life nor yet the crown of righteousness. The Apostle warns us not to be influenced in our service by "filthy lucre," and he adds, "When the chief Shepherd shall appear, ye shall receive a crown of glory that fadeth not away." Ah! if you to-day and all your days, are sweetly looking in the calm rest of the faith of Christ upon the past, that is yours! A cup of cold water, given in the name of a disciple, shall in no wise lose its reward.

If in the Church of Christ you are tending the lambs; if you are watching over those new born souls; if you are seeking to instruct the ignorant, and if you are entirely developing the love of God, oh! how that chief Shepherd will bless you! how He waits to put the crown of glory upon your head. This crown you see is in connection with distinguished service in the Church of Christ. Daniel says, "Many of them that sleep in the dust of the earth shall awake, some to everlasting life, and some to shame and everlasting contempt; and they that be wise shall shine as the brightness of the firmament; and they that turn many to righteousness, as the stars for ever and ever." I sometimes think, in one sense I shall never know to thank God enough for converting me when but a boy of fifteen. Oh! when I think of men converted at fifty and sixty! How little of life is left to them! They have no vigorous manhood to bring and lay upon the altar. But blessed be His name, His grace will receive and say of each one, "He hath done—she hath done what she could." Oh! how

immensely important it is to see that our life here
is like a great seed ground, in which we place the
acts of a devoted life to bear fruit that shall be as
an eternal heritage in the kingdom of God!

I beseech you to be watchful. Christianity is
not exhausted when you become a Christian, —
you have only begun. It is a life of endless progression. Paul reproves the Corinthians for going
to law before the world, instead of before the
Church, and says : 'Have ye no wise men among
you? Don't you know that the saints are to judge
the world?' 'Don't you know,' again he asks,
'that the saints are to judge the world?' Oh!
God, am I to be Thy executor in reference to the
judgment of the ungodly? Am I, by Thy grace, to
occupy the judicial bench in company with Christ,
as touching Thy final designs? Are angels that
kept not their first estate, to hear their sentence
from these lips? Then, what a fool that man must
be who fails to recognize the wonderful fact that
Christians will be "kings and priests unto God forever!" It is a wonderful thing to be a Christian.

There is one other thought I would just speak
to you about before I close. The Apostle calls
Christians his crown of righteousness. Ah! sirs,
some of you, I fear, will claim starless crowns.
You have had the opportunity of winning your
brother for Christ, but by your half heedlessness
you have lost the opportunity. Mothers, you might
have saved your children for Christ, but in your
coldness you let them grow until the evil days
came when they had no pleasure in the Lord. A

few weeks before I left England I came in contact with one of the most melancholy cases of that kind, I think, I ever heard of. In a little town in Suffolk county, a little boy died, and he said to his father and mother: "You have been good parents to me from my earliest memory until now. I never wanted for anything. But your relationship to me has just been restricted to my body. You have never said one word to me about my soul, and I am dying and am lost."

Oh! 'tis terrible to think that we who have the light of life should actually refuse to shine. It is not that we have not the light. This is what Christ says to us: "Let your light shine." You have it,—He says, "Let it." You have hidden it under a bushel of shame,—you have hidden its brightness, unlike the Apostle Paul, who says: 'I am debtor both to the Greeks and to the barbarians; the sinner, the bond and the free, wherefore my life may be rich.' Oh! I beg of you, enter into the kingdom of God. I remember grasping the hand of a brother who died,—a member of my church at Notting Hill. He said to me: "Dear sir, I am going home," and looking up in my face with his bright eyes, for he was dying of consumption, he said: "Sir, I shall be on the look-out for you when you come." Ay:—

" Teachers and kindred have passed on before,
Waiting, they watch us approaching the shore."

Have you no interest in laying up for time to come? That quaint old preacher,—strong, vigorous man as he was, — Ralph Erskine, had in his congregation a very rich, but very godless man. Often reproved, this godless man died, and one of his friends came to Erskine, and said, "Sir, So-and-so's dead." Erskine could be very sarcastic when he pleased, and he said, "Is he?" "Yes," said his friend, "and he has died worth a hundred thousand pounds." "Um!" says Erskine in his gruff way, "that's a nice sum of money to begin business with, in the next world." Gold is not the currency of that country. See to it, I beseech you, that you lay up for yourselves that which shall make the Master say to you, 'Well done ; thou hast been faithful over a few things, have thou authority over ten cities.'

Oh! Master, what does that mean? Are we in the ages to come, in consonance with our kingly character, sharers of Thy throne, to have the government of the eternal angels? Are we to have sovereignties that shall put the petty sovereignties of the world into the shade as something mean and contemptible? Ah! it may be even so! The outlook of the Christian is so magnificent that my poor speech and thought are not fitted to set it forth. May God help us, that we lose not a full reward.

And now here are words of solemn rebuke from God to those cold-hearted Christians who sit down in indolence and sloth, and who do not hesitate to make light of God's honest servants. They will come and look in at an inquiry meeting, and brand it as some social excitement. Alas!

alas! they have never had any interest in saving
souls, and unless they get repentant and broken
hearts, — for I am free to confess that I have done
most of my repentance since I was converted, yes,
I mean what I say, I have done most of my repentance since I became a converted man, — unless
they change their minds, and their hearts are
broken about this, the day of the Lord will declare
that though they themselves may be saved, it will
be "so as by fire," and instead of having crowns to
cast at His feet, their hands will be empty. I care
most for the crowns for their intrinsic worth. I
thank God it is written, — for when I have read
about the crowns, I have wondered what I should
do with them, — I thank God that I read: "They
cast them at His feet." I would like to do that.

Oh! I charge you see to it that you be not saved
by the skin of your teeth. See to it that the angels
do not have to challenge you; but that adding to
your faith virtue, to virtue knowledge, to knowledge
temperance, to temperance patience, to patience
godliness, to godliness brotherly kindness, and to
brotherly kindness love, even so you shall not be
barren nor unfruitful in the knowledge of our Lord,
but entrance shall be abundantly administered unto
you in the everlasting kingdom of our Lord, not in
the future only but now. As the Master says,
"Except a corn of wheat fall into the ground and
die, it abideth alone: but if it die, it bringeth forth
much fruit." I hear men saying sometimes — they
have said said it to me again and again, — "Ah! sir,
you are killing yourself." I tell them I mean to

die in the service of Christ. By His grace it will be said, that this life was sacrificed, if you will call it so, in His service. When I see a man sacrificing his life for money, do you think I would allow him to call me a fool? The folly is his! When I see a man sacrificing his life for sensuality, what more pitiful folly can there be than his?

Oh! brethren and sisters, I commend this subject to you, and I pray that you may have many sheaves to lay at the feet of the great Husbandman, as James puts it, who quietly waits for the fruits of the earth. God bless these words to you, and may they be productive of intelligent devotion and service, and may you see that Christ's life is not a thing of traditions. Remember that the service of Christ demands every power you possess, in the spirit of love. I would that you should realize this. I fear that very many Christians understand but little of the power of the services of love. My brethren, bear with a plain illustration; it is intended to carry weight with it, and it is forcible. If the time should come when any woman in this room should be betrothed to the man of her choice, she would not be a woman if she did not allow her heart to go to him. And mark you, if you are betrothed to Christ, let your heart go to Him not as a Master but as a Husband; let your free spirit rejoice in His service.

I know of many Christians working hard, oh! so hard! And what do they do? They crowd their service with acts of work in order to make out that they are God's children. Oh! it would make me sorrowful, if, when I reached England, I saw my daughter working hard at her studies from six o'clock in the morning until nine at night; and when I asked her, "What is all this work for, dear child?" she should look up in my eyes and say, "I am trying to establish in my heart that I am your own child." I would say, "What! working fifteen hours a day to establish in your own mind your relationship to me! Oh! never do that, you *are* my child." The idea of a servile spirit in the child of God is terrible. Let your hearts go to Him, and you know how easy it is to serve those we love.

ABIDING IN CHRIST.

JOHN xv. 4.

ABIDE IN ME, AND I IN YOU. AS THE BRANCH CANNOT BEAR FRUIT OF ITSELF, EXCEPT IT ABIDE IN THE VINE ; NO MORE CAN YE, EXCEPT YE ABIDE IN ME.

THERE must ever be a great difference between our knowledge and our realized experience ; but I am persuaded that the gulf need not be astonishingly deep, and while our knowledge should ever be in advance of our experience, yet I am sure of this, that the Lord wants us to know the power of that endless life that we possess, from the first dawn of our waking consciousness in the morning, until we lose ourselves in sleep at night. I am the more anxious to say this, because I do not wish to discourage the least of God's little ones. I am anxious to say it, lest any of us should suppose that we have obtained a position where there is no future advancement. I trust that we deeply feel to-day, — perhaps more than ever, — the Apostle's words, 'Forgetting the things which are behind, and reaching forth unto those things which are before, we press toward the mark,' for the prize of the high calling of God encourages us.

I wish to read to you now a few verses from the fifteenth chapter of John, and I will be very thankful if you will have your Bibles open before you as I read. [The speaker here read from the first to the sixteenth verse of the fifteenth chapter of St. John's Gospel, both inclusive, and then proceeded:] I will stay our reading there. The words to which I call your attention are found at the commencement of the fourth verse, "Abide in Me, and I in you." Very wonderful is the testimony of Jesus. In the preceding chapter this question is put to Him: Judas (not Iscariot) said, "Lord, how is it that Thou wilt manifest Thyself unto us, and not unto the world? Jesus answered and said unto him, If a man love Me, he will keep My words."

"If a man love Me," observe, "he will keep My words: and My Father will love him, and we will come unto him, and make our abode with him." Now, it seems a wonderful thing to say that the renewed heart of every child of God is the home of the living God, but I dare not deny it: I should not be faithful to my precious Lord, if I did not affirm that there is *not one* of them in whom the Father and the Son alike have not come to make their abode. God help us to receive that thought. And again: "Your bodies are the temples of the Holy Ghost." Will you be careful of that — the Trinity enshrined within us. Oh! Emmanuel, God with us, how wonderful is Thine intention to the sons of men! That is the human side of it.

You will find the divine side in the last verse of the second chapter of Ephesians. When you read these words, speaking of the Church of God, let me remind you that it consists not of professed members of any order of Christians, nor yet of any " section," as they call it; no, but of the living members of the living body in every department of God's great family: "In whom all the building fitly framed together groweth unto a holy temple in the Lord. In whom ye also are builded together for a habitation of God through the Spirit." This is the divine side. What a wonderful thing it is to say in this sense, God is homeless!! But yet it is true. The highest thought of God as touching His home, has not yet been consummated, but it is being wrought out even now in the world, "builded together for a habitation of God through the Spirit."

Well, now, it may perhaps be asked by some of you, "What is it to abide in Christ?" I am thankful that in such a theme as this the Scripture is its own interpreter, and let me remind you that this has evidently been God's thought from the commencement. When He redeemed Israel He did not redeem them into circumstances of independence; on the contrary, He redeemed them into circumstances of dependence upon Himself. He made them His especial care, — He was their king. When He selected Abraham, He told him as one of the conditions of the divine friendship, that he should leave his own kindred and his own home ; and he was separated as a stranger and a pilgrim, and it is said that "he looked for a city which hath foundations, whose builder and maker is God." And so on through the whole range of the former testimony you will come in contact with these words.

Take David as an example, — he said : "I was glad when they said unto me, Let us go unto the house of the Lord." "My heart and my flesh crieth out for the living God." "How amiable are thy tabernacles, O Lord of hosts." But since Jesus came, the material has given place to the spiritual. It is not in temples made with hands; it is not in Shiloh, nor yet at Jerusalem, that the tabernacle of God is with men. The Christ of God is come, and is not enshrined beneath majestic cathedral domes, but in His own beautiful manhood, that He may get into the hearts of men. Oh! precious truth, — the passing away of the material, the incoming of the loving, mighty heart of Jesus enshrined in a body like ours.

I wish you to notice that Jesus, in speaking of abiding in Him, tells us what this is in four special ways in this chapter; and if you will first of all look at the ninth verse, you will see the first thought that I will give you: "As the Father hath loved me, so have I loved you : continue ye in my love." Now if I am asked what it is to abide in Christ, I say to you it is to abide in His love. Mark the first of these words. It is not our love to Christ,—it is Christ's love to us. I confess that I have been ashamed of my love to Christ thousands of times ; I have never once been ashamed of His love to me.

I was much impressed when preaching in my native village three or four years ago, with the remark of an aged man present in the congregation. He was over ninety, and had known me when I was but a very little boy, and he spoke to me, and I asked him this question, "My dear aged friend, do you love Jesus?" His deeply furrowed face was lit up with a smile that sixty-seven years of discipleship had imparted, and grasping my hand with both his, he said, "Oh ! I can tell you something better than that." I asked him, "What is that?" "Oh! sir," he said, "He loves me." The old man was right, it is the love of Jesus ; and Jesus asks us to continue in His love, — that love which is everlasting, that love which is boundless, that love which reaches on and on throughout the eternity of the future.

Blessed thought this, Christ says, "As the Father hath loved Me, so have I loved you." I ask you where is the line that can gauge this? Stand and pause. Let the Master's sweet voice reach us. Spirit of God, strengthen us that we may understand it. "As the Father hath loved Me, so have I loved you." Is that the measure? Oh! ineffable love of God to Thine only begotten Son! And dost Thou, Jesus, love me like that? Then in that love will I abide; I will not look at the little I know of it. A dear child in London went with his father for the first time to Brighton, and when the

4*

little fellow came home, he said to one of his school-mates who was in the house, "I have seen the sea." The little boy was pleased with what he had seen; but his father overhearing him thought, "How little of the sea my boy has seen; just to the sky-line round there, that was all." Some of us who have been to Australia a hundred days out of sight of land could say we had seen the sea, and I sometimes think that when by faith we get out of the shallows, where we lose sight of land, calmly riding on the bosom of the mighty heights and depths and lengths and breadths of the love of Christ, we then see the sea.

"Abide in My love." Oh! brethren, this is rest. I was remarking in the prayer-meeting this morning, that I very much wished Christians would let alone the miserable talk about trying to love Christ. There is not a husband in this house who would not be pained to his heart's centre, — I know I should, — if he had been absent from his wife for a week or ten days, and she should say to him on his return, "I have been trying to love you since you went away." Love is not a force-pump; you cannot get it up that way. I beseech you, let alone trying to love Christ; let it alone until the generous glow of His love begets the generous return tide of your own.

I once heard a brother say, in one of the Dublin meetings: "Worship in its highest sense is this, the heart filled with God's goodness, and hence filled with His love and power until we cannot hold that which we have, and we send the overflow back

again to the Eternal." It is very true. That is
one of the highest thoughts of all that you can have
of what worship is. My time forbids me to enlarge
upon this.

Will you now just notice the eleventh verse:
"These things have I spoken unto you that my joy
might remain in you, and that your joy might be
full." And here again see how Christ maintains
the same order. It is not your joy that increases,
— it is Christ's joy in you. I beg you get clear
thoughts of Scripture, — get on to God's foundations, or you never can have a superstructure
that is worth looking at. You call in a builder and
you ask him to rear you a house of four or five
stories on one of your loamy, sandy foundations;
and I warrant you the worse your foundation, the
worse your superstructure will look when it is up;
it will be full of cracks here and there. Your
superstructure must be built on God's foundation.
Christ's love first, and then that that followeth out
of it. "Abide in My love," in My joy. I often
quote those words to dear friends in England which
we read in the thirteenth of Luke: "There is joy
in the presence of the angels of God over one sinner that repenteth," and nearly all the Christians
that I come into contact with, immediately identify
those words with the angels' joy. Why, my friends,
it does not say so. It says there is joy "*in the
presence* of angels," and if you asked me whose joy
it is, I would not affirm that the angels are not con-
tributors to that joy as friends and neighbors, but
it is the joy of the Father—of Him who gave His

precious Son. It is the harvest joy from the earth that makes glad God's heart. Let me read to you one passage that you will find in the prophet Zephaniah. They call him a minor prophet, I suppose, because he did not write as much as some of the other prophets, but what he has written is very blessed: "The Lord thy God in the midst of thee is mighty; He will save; He will rejoice over thee with joy; He will rest in His love; He will joy over thee with singing."

I remember being at Brighton one day, — I was very weary with preaching, — and as I walked out on the dyke road, that some of you may know, my hat in my hand, in the beautiful May morning so fresh and clear, the gladsome breeze so grateful to my hot forehead, I looked on the scene around me and thought how fair it was. There was the green verdure of God's carpet at my feet, those grand old hills right and left giving such a view of His power, the bright sunshine overhead, and yonder, away in the distance, the bright blue sea. And as I looked over it I thought, what a grand theatre is this for the display of God's power. But I asked myself, Is there anything in all this that makes glad the heart of God? Does the sunshine cause Him joy? Do these grand old mountains move one emotion of the mighty God? And I felt that it could not be — that God's emotions are not moved by the material world. You must go into the divine word to find what God needs in this respect. John says, "God is love," and the waves of ocean cannot satisfy His want, — He wants our love. But in the great theatre of countless millions of human hearts God finds the place where His requirements are met; and I venture to affirm that this is the reason why, when the disciples came back, after leaving Jesus at the well of Samaria tired and worn, and said to Him: "Master, eat," that He turned to them and said: "I have meat to eat that ye know not of." Peter asked: "Hath any man brought Him aught to eat?" I think if I had been there I would have said: "No, Peter, no; but this dear woman, for whose love Jesus came from heaven, has just sent the first tide of her new-born love into His heart, and His hunger is past and His thirst is gone," for it was His meat and drink to find the salvation of men. But there is a capability that you and I possess, if we rest in His joy, as the bride in the arms of her husband. You sing:—

> "Safe in the arms of Jesus,
> Safe on His gentle breast."

Is this mere hollow sentiment, or is it true? God enable you to abide in His joy. And yet again, in the fifteenth verse: "I call you not servants; for the servant knoweth not what his lord doeth: but I have called you friends." It is not that I have called Jesus my friend, it is that He hath called me His friend,— He is responsible for that. You have no business to find fault with Him for doing it. If He is pleased to call a poor sinner like me His friend, that is His business, — you have no right to object to it. Oh! how precious! But I venture to say this: I would not take to my

grey-headed father to-day, and present as my
friend, a young man of whose moral character I
was ashamed, and I speak it with profound meaning when I affirm that this expression involves that
Jesus has caused to pass away from us as His,
everything that would prevent His presenting us
to His Father as His friends. Do you believe that
Fit for His friendship ! "He that sanctifieth and
they who are sanctified are all one, for which cause
He is not ashamed to call them brethren, — friends.
Take the next verse: "Ye have not chosen Me, but
I have chosen you," and here again the same sweet
thought appears, — not our choice of Christ but
Christ's choice of us. Oh! how precious.

I have used an illustration that I might repeat
here to you. It has been said by some one, in a
kind of parable : " Supposing that a flock of sheep
were to come to the shepherd, and one of the sheep
should say to the shepherd, ' Shepherd, I know that
I am your sheep, for you got eight pounds of wool
off my back at last shearing day ;' and another
were to come and say, ' Shepherd, I believe that I
am your sheep, too, because you got six pounds of
wool from my back,' and another were to come and
say, ' Well, and I suppose that I must be your
sheep, too, because you got four pounds of wool
from mine,' and a fourth were to come and say,
' Really, I am in doubt, for you only got two pounds
of wool off my back;' until at length," says the
writer of this parable, "one poor scraggy fellow
came along and said, 'I do not know whether I am
your sheep, because you did not get anything from

my back.' But supposing that the shepherd turned and said : ' I would that every one of you gave me eight pounds of wool: but the question whether you are my sheep or not rests here — that I bought you and paid for you.'" Oh ! blessed truth ! Yes, we have not chosen Him, but " I have chosen you and ordained you that ye should go and bring forth fruit and that your fruit should remain."

Look at these four things, love, joy, friendship, choice. I am not about to enlarge upon them ; I might with profit, but I will not. I remember, — you will forgive me, I am sure, for the personal allusion, — I remember how, when this heart of mine first loved an earthly object very dear to me, I was very poor and went away to Australia to get what we sometimes call a start in the world ; and when I look upon my beloved wife to-day, I think of her from this point of view, my life, my joy, my friend, my choice ; and ours is a happy home. If you know this — if it is reality to you, — you will rest in His love. Why, He "joys over thee with singing." Yes, 'tis even thus, — married to Him, the object of His eternal love, His abiding joy, His unchanging friendship, His choice.

But I dare not part with you thus. It is only one side of my theme. For these wonderful spiritual blessings there is a corresponding responsibility on our part, and how sweet is the teaching of Jesus, that there is responsibility. I don't want men to talk glibly about the choice of Christ. If you speak about His election, remember that it is "unto obedience and sprinkling of the blood of

Jesus Christ." Remember that we are redeemed to be "a peculiar people." I think if there is one type of Christianity so-called, more terrible than another, it is that in which a man settles down into some cold, intellectual understanding of the truth, and says he is saved when his life declares that he is lost. That I deprecate. I thank God from the depths of my heart, that the Father of our spirits, the God of truth, when men have gone to one extreme, has supplied them with correctives on the other side.

Now look at this tenth verse again. It shows you the human responsibility. "If ye keep My commandments, ye shall abide in My love; even as I have kept My Father's commandments, and abide in His love." This, then, is to be the test of your rest in the love of Christ. If you refuse to keep His commandments, you shall not know His love. I remember once hearing a minister, who was speaking of the indwelling of the Spirit, use the following beautiful figure: "Take care," said he, "that as your body is the temple of the Holy Ghost, He has the whole range of the house; if you shut up the drawing room of the soul" — that was his thoughtful expression — "for worldly company, and you go in and fraternize with them, I do not say that the Spirit will leave the house — very faithfulness to Christ will prevent that — but like a grieved guest, He will go to some upper chamber in the soul, and He will leave you to your worldly company."

It is even so. Many of you here, I fear, have

again and again grieved the Spirit of God by giving
yourselves up to fellowships, by giving yourselves
up to associations in the world, which you knew
had no power in the kingdom of God; for "The
kingdom of God is not meat and drink." It is not
your showy dress dinners; it is not your ball-room
splendor; it is not the gilded halls of the theatre—
no, brethren, a thousand times no! "but righteousness and joy and peace in the Holy Ghost." Take
care where you put that redeemed body. Will you
carry it inside the theatre, redeemed young sister?
Beware lest you change the character of the Spirit
from an abiding Comforter into a constant reprover.
There are many Christians who know the Spirit of
God mainly as a reprover of them "all along the
line" of their life.

Notice again, "His commandments are not
grievous." Listen:—"Oh Israel, that thou hadst
hearkened unto My commandments, then had thy
peace been as a river, and thy righteousness as the
waves of the sea." Now, side by side with the joy,
we have the "new commandment." What is that?
I believe that that joy is the highest spiritual
blessing that we know. I believe that joy is in
relation to love, what the ripe fruit is in relation to
the blossom. It is the ripening of love. Now, if
you desire to obtain this highest blessing, the prize
that you must hope for is the love of God's people
of every name. "Seeing ye have purified your souls
in obeying the truth through the Spirit, see that
ye love one another with a pure heart fervently."
You want Christ's joy; then I tell you that you

must love your fellow Christians of every name,
not in word but in deed and in practice. You are
not to love your fellow Christians because they are
not members of the church that you attend, nor
yet because of the social position that you occupy.

If you have sisters in the church who are not so
rich as you, you must not pass them by. You
must love. Oh, the curse of those opinions that
have separated God's children one from another.
I have learned this, that names have little power ;
yet there is a name that makes us know what love
is,—"Jesus," who loved us and gave Himself for us,
and I would rather be stoned to death, than refuse
to go out in all that means the bigness of the
Master's love, to every one — even the least of His
little ones. Would you abide in His joy? Then
you must give up that narrow self-consciousness.
"Master, we saw one casting out devils in Thy
name, and we forbade him, because he followed not
us." "Forbid him not." Oh! these distinctions!
We have a great deal of pride in England. You
know that two of the coins that we have in currency
there are the half-crown and the two-shilling piece.
I used these once in speaking of this pride, and
said, "So petty are the distinctions amongst many
Christians, that Mrs. Half Crown will scarcely
speak to Mrs. Florin." It is just the same else-
where.

I tell you, brethren, that I do not believe the
Gospel reduces everything to one common level,
but that it brings character up to the dignity of
that hearty generous love that suffers long, love

that is kind, love that thinks no evil. A great deal
of the love that I see amongst so-called Christians
fails very quickly. That is not the love of the
thirteenth chapter of First Corinthians. If you
would abide in His joy, you must love His people.
I met a poor fellow who was converted at fifty. I
was converted at fifteen. Sin never had the power
over me that it has had over him for many years.
Am I to put the standard as high for him as for
myself? Shame on me if I do. Am I to point the
finger at him? Oh! brethren, may God send home
these thoughts to your hearts.

And now, once more, as touching the friendship,
what is involved? what is the correlative on the
human side? "All things that I have heard of My
Father, I have made known unto you." You must
make that book your closest companion. I say it
not to make you think anything of me, but that is
the most intimate companion I have ; not even my
own precious wife do I know so intimately as the
book of God. No ; that I should be a husband is
one of the happinesses of my life ; that I should be
a father or a preacher is one of those incidents that
come along, but the *fact* of my existence is, that I
should be a friend of Christ, and possess the knowledge of His love. How often I go into houses and
see the big Bible lying there—you can see it is not
a used book. I have seen, in my Bible readings in
England, ladies in the upper and middle classes,
and accomplished women by hundreds, come in,
and when I have got them to this point, that they
have brought their Bibles with them, they have not

known where to look for the Epistle to the Romans, and I have seen them turning over in the Old Testament for it. The ignorance of God's word is profound, and I wonder not that they could have so little of what is meant by friendship. "Oh! So-and-so's a very intimate friend of mine," says one, "but we only see one another once in six months, not oftener than that." Why, that would be a contradiction in terms. Is an intimate friend one who has *met* you? No, certainly not; but one whom you have companioned with.

And now, what is the last responsibility? "Ye have not chosen Me, but I have chosen you, and ordained you, that ye should go and bring forth fruit, and that your fruit should remain." For fruit-bearing, brethren : remember that, *fruit-bearing.* I believe that this is where our safety lies when people speak to us as they sometimes do about perfection. If I went into a vineyard or an orchard and saw there a tree full of corrupt fruit, taking off every particle of that fruit would not make the tree good. Some people have an idea that it is only necessary to pull off the bad things — the unfruitful works of darkness—and I press that word unfruitful. Mark what that word is! The Christian is not a tree like the oak tree ; he is rather like an apple tree. I would have every branch of my life loaded with fruit.

On my way down to Bristol, I stepped out of the train at a little town where I was to preach one night. There was on the station a rustic seat, and growing over it there was a small tree — the

station-master was evidently a man of taste, for
there were many beautiful flowers about the station
— and in order to incline the boughs so as to form
an arch over the seat, he had tied many stones on
the branches. I observed that it was not a fruit-
bearing tree; and I believe many Christians are
like that. God has inclined the branches of their
life in the direction He wanted, but alas! alas!
they give themselves up rather to please themselves
than to bear fruit unto Him, and so He has come
and tied the heavy stones of care and troubles,
and what you call afflictions, to them in order to
bring them where He wants them. Fruit-bearing
is not the thing that some people would make it.

Suppose that I had here to-day a beautiful purple
cluster of grapes, such as you know grow in England, and such as I presume you have here, and
supposing I were to look at that splendid cluster
and say: "How did you ever come into that beautiful condition? What ripeness! What fullness!
How luscious! How beautiful is the bloom upon
you! How fair you look! How did you come into
this condition?" The cluster might be supposed
to answer: "Oh! I simply abided in the vine."
"And how is that; did you not go out into activi-
ties?" "Oh! no; I simply abided in the vine and
out of the reach of the frosts; it was by virtue of
my place in the vine that I attained to what I am."
No thanks to ourselves, — we are silent. Our only
praise is of Him whose virtue we have received
until we have come to the condition in which you
see us. 'Tis ever thus, oh! fruit-bearer. As He

5

says: "Without Me ye can do nothing." Would God that you might form the solemn resolution: "Jesus, Thou sayest, 'Without Me ye can do nothing,' and I will enter into my side of that contract: and that is this, Lord I will do nothing without Thee, — it shall be Thy love, Thy sympathy, Thy strength, — not I, but Christ living in me."

"Abide in Me and I in you," and a generous fruit shall come morning, noon and night, and thine old age shall be blessed. "Thou shalt still bring forth fruit in old age, and be fat and flourishing," for "Herein is my Father glorified that ye bear much fruit." Remember it, — love, joy, friendship, choice, — and the responsibilities, take thought of them. Keep His commandments, love His people, search His word, bring forth fruit, and thou shalt understand, not in theory only, but in actual experience, what it is to "Abide in Me and I in you." Amen.

THE

MINISTRY OF THE SPIRIT.

ROMANS VIII. 14.

FOR AS MANY AS ARE LED BY THE SPIRIT OF GOD, THEY ARE
THE SONS OF GOD.

PERHAPS it would be helpful to you, brethren,
if I were to speak to you upon the ministry
of the Spirit. Let us turn to the sixteenth
chapter of the Gospel of John, fifth, sixth and
seventh verses. "But now I go My way to Him
that sent Me; and none of you asketh Me, Whither
goest Thou? But because I have said these things
unto you, sorrow hath filled your heart. Nevertheless I tell you the truth; It is expedient for you
that I go away: for if I go not away, the Comforter
will not come unto you; but if I depart, I will send
Him unto you." I intend to emphasize the personal
pronouns that follow, and for the simple reason,
that in our day there are a great many who think
of the Spirit as an influence. Now, I beg of you,
banish such a thought from your minds. I never

like to speak about the influences of the Spirit of
God. It is an unscriptural term. Of course, I
know what it means, but there is nothing in the
Spirit less than this, the power. As though Jesus
had foreseen the danger that is suggested by this
thought, observe how He emphasizes what comes
after.

" And when He is come, He will reprove the world of sin,
and of righteousness, and of judgment: Of sin, because they
believe not on me; Of righteousness, because I go to My
Father, and ye see Me no more; Of judgment, because the
prince of this world is judged. I have yet many things to
say unto you, but ye cannot bear them now. Howbeit, when
He, the Spirit of truth, is come, He will guide you into all
truth: for He shall not speak of Himself; but whatsoever He
shall hear, that shall He speak: and He will show you things
to come. He shall glorify Me: for He shall receive of Mine,
and shall show it unto you."

I thank Jesus for this splendid specimen of tau-
tology, to rebuke the skepticism of the day, that
would talk about the Spirit of God as an influence.
"Grieve not the Holy Spirit of God," saith Paul.
Who ever talks about grieving an influence? What
nonsense! We speak of grieving a friend; we talk
of grieving some loved one — grieve an influence
indeed! What rubbish! Brethren, I speak solemn
words to you about this. The Spirit of God is a
person equally with Christ. May I ask you now to
turn over to the second chapter of the Acts of the
Apostles. [Having read that chapter down to the
thirty-third verse inclusive, the speaker went on to
say:] It was necessary that I should read thus far,
contrary to my desire, in order to point out to

you, that while the Spirit of God has ever been
in the Church, was with the Church in its earliest
days, as it is written, "In the beginning * * * the
Spirit of God moved upon the face of the waters"
—in the book of Genesis; seen in increasing
brightness as we hear the Psalmist say: "Take
not Thy Holy Spirit from me;" wonderfully clear
in the testimony of Ezekiel, when he said, "Come
from the four winds, O breath! and breathe upon
these slain, that they may live;" ever carrying on
with increasing power the great work of gathering
together, from Abel's time until now, the great
family of the living God.

It remained, however, for the Lord Jesus Christ
to come, and it remained for Him to be exalted
before we became possessed of the Comforter—the
fullness. However blessed the Holy Ghost may
have been known in individual experience in the
times that are past, never let us lose sight of this
great truth spoken by Christ, prophetic of His
glory in the seventh chapter of John. " He that
believeth on Me, as the Scripture hath said, out of
his [inmost being or] belly shall flow rivers of living
water. (But this spake He of the Spirit, which
they that believe on Him should receive: for the
Holy Ghost was not yet given ; because that Jesus
was not yet glorified.)" But now He is glorified—
exalted to the Father's right hand. "He hath shed
forth this that ye now see and hear."

Oh! with what divinest intention did Jesus tell
His disciples to tarry at Jerusalem until they were
endued with power from on high! The Saviour's

ministry on earth being finished, His place is as a forerunner at the right hand of God, waiting to introduce those who come as the great harvest from earth, and it remained for the Spirit of God to perpetuate the work of Jesus. And I desire to express a thought which I feel will carry your judgment with me, when I say, that whether you think of the dignity of Christ's character, or whether you contemplate the great issues intended, the work of Christ must—mark what I say—*must* pass into the hands of the Spirit of God. Shall the magnificent issues of Christ's work come into the hands of fitful and spasmodic and uncertain men? Surely not. We could not entertain such a thought for a moment. The Spirit of God alone has dignity enough, has power enough. Who can raise the dead but the Spirit of God? who but the Spirit of God can bring men from darkness to light? Oh! brethren, I confess to you that I should give up the ministry before I am a week older, were it not for the profound consciousness that I am aided by God's Spirit. I tell you, I have but very little hope of any man who disdains or insults the Spirit of grace.

If any man affect to believe that his intellect is enough to receive divine truth without the Spirit, I believe that man will die and be lost as surely as that I am standing on this platform. These are solemn words, but remember that the work contemplated by the preaching of the Gospel is work for eternity, and we want an eternal Builder to fashion the stones.

Jesus puts, as it were, a stay to all active efforts. He tells His disciples, the one hundred and twenty, to wait,—here let me say that I have no sympathy with those who tell us that the one hundred and twenty represented the results of Christ's ministry upon earth,—because, in the fifteenth of First Corinthians Paul tells us that He was seen by above five hundred, and I believe that in Judea there were tens of thousands, the fruits of Christ's labors. It may be a new idea to some of you, but I ask you to think about it and read in the light of God's Word whether it be not so.

They were to wait. I see that gathered company of the disciples in the upper chamber, abstracting themselves from the affairs of life as much as possible. They were to wait until the day of Pentecost came,—until it came fully,—and they patiently waited. They were gainers by waiting. I tell you that it is a very blessed thing to wait before God until we get the noise and bustle out of us.

It is written of Christ: "He shall not cry, nor lift up nor cause His voice to be heard in the street," and I do fear that many Christians are living such busy lives that they have too much noise about them to hear the voice of Jesus. John himself learned in that upper room that it was not by love alone. Peter, with all his desire to redeem the past, he too, must learn that it was not by the zeal that should animate him. No; I think the lesson that they were learning was but this : " Not by might, nor by power, but by My Spirit, saith the Lord of hosts."

The current of the divine Spirit's purposes is flowing through this world to-day. If you cast yourselves into its flow, you will fulfill the will of God, but everything depends on that. If you stand aside, you will not do it; you cannot do it; it is impossible to do it. O God, bring us into Thy will in this respect, we beseech Thee. Now, there is a very beautiful teaching in the gift of Pentecost. You remember how on the first day of the resurrection, Jesus said to Mary, "Touch Me not: for I have not yet ascended unto My Father: but go to my brethren, and say unto them, I ascend unto My Father, and your Father; and to My God, and your God." Now, I venture to think, without at all dogmatizing, that the first thing Jesus did on the morning of the resurrection, was to present Himself in the presence of the Father. Of course, you know after the resurrection, Jesus' body was not subject to material laws as it had been before. It is an interesting thought — that He could give Himself to the apostles, and say, "Handle Me and see, for a spirit hath not flesh and bones," and then vanish out of sight. Time and space were nothing. It was simply the action of His will; and I believe He was in the presence of His Father on the resurrection morning, presenting His credentials from the earth.

That which suggested this thought to my mind is found in the book of Leviticus,* where on the morrow after the Passover Sabbath the high priest is directed to present a green sheaf out of the harvest

* . See Chapter xxiii. 10th and following verses.

field before the Lord. You will find that the difference between the feast of the Passover and the feast of weeks was exactly fifty days.

Forty days was Christ with the apostles after His resurrection, engaged in establishing them in the things relating to His kingdom, until His ascension ; and I have no doubt the remaining ten days while they were waiting for His promised gift of the Spirit, were occupied in the same way. Thus the forty and the ten, like the time which the Jews were commanded to count "from the morrow after the Sabbath, from the day that" they "brought the sheaf of the wave offering, * * * even unto the morrow after the seventh Sabbath, number fifty days ; and when the fifty days were up, I see the Father, having accepted Him, giving Him the wonderful gift of the Holy Ghost. That is our royal heritage. I do not receive the Holy Ghost merely because I am fit for it, but I receive the gift of the Holy Ghost because Christ is exalted. I ask you to think of that.

The Apostle says, "This only would I learn of you, Received ye the Spirit by the works of the law or by the hearing of faith?" You believe, and you receive this gift by faith only. Now, I want you to notice some precious teaching here. I see that gathered company in the upper chamber, and when the morning of Pentecost is come, Jesus receiving that gift which is the fullness of love and joy and peace and every blessing, and in the impetuosity of His great love, sending that Spirit down "suddenly." Oh! mark the impetuosity of His love.

" Suddenly there came a sound from heaven as of a rushing mighty wind." He had told them that He would not leave them comfortless. Those were almost His last words, and just as He told them at the table, " I will not drink henceforth of this fruit of the vine, until that day when I drink it new with you in My Father's kingdom."

The grand cluster from this earthly Eschol went up, and expressed as it were in the Father's presence the purity of His glorious and wondrous manhood, and then the cup of our salvation from that expressed individuality comes down to be gladness and rejoicing in the Church of the living God. Let us take that cup of salvation. It is put into our hands, let us drink it, and magnify Him who hath given it in His wonderful grace. I am not surprised that they said "These men are drunk with new wine." It seems to me, that with the light of the Epistles if I had been there, I should have said, ' Yes, we accept what you say; we are full of new wine.' We are to be inflamed, to be excited, to be energized by the Spirit.

There is a sense in which our life is not a stagnant thing. Some one has said, that man's life is passed between these two points, desire and satiety. There is a great deal of truth in this, and so I remind you here to-day, that the Spirit of God has been given to us to inflame us, to excite us, to be to us what the sensual man finds in the wine cup. See him, mark his eye, look at his gait, listen to his speech. He will speak as he cannot speak, he will go where he would not go, except under this influ-

ence. There is an unnatural brilliancy about his
eye. But this drunkenness of the disciples was
not an impure thing, but a power, an energy, the
energy of the Holy Ghost. God grant that you and
I may work in the power of the new, the true, the
beautiful, as Paul puts it, "Striving according to His
working which worketh in me mightily." It is the
Spirit of might.

Will you notice again, that the Spirit is represented here like cloven tongues of fire. It is a
very beautiful expression. I believe that the lesson
taught by the impartation of the Spirit, enabling
the disciples to teach the Parthians and the Medes
and the Elamites and all the other different nation-
alities that were gathered together, so that there
was not a creed outside the range of their teaching,
— is, that in all the departments of life we may
glorify God. For instance, I am here a preacher
of the gospel; if I return to England, I take the
place of pastor of my church ; I am a father, a
husband, a business man, and the Spirit of God
has been given, that in all these details of my life
I may glorify Him ; for observe, "Whether therefore ye eat, or drink, or whatsoever ye do, do all
to the glory of God." I believe that the Spirit of
God—and I say it with thoughtfulness—is needed
perhaps more in the market than anywhere else.
In the counting-house, in the different spheres of
every-day life, it is needed. It is not in some official
position as a rule, that we feel its want, but where
there is failure in what are sometimes called the
little things.

The Spirit of God can endow you with a wonderful inheritance. There is a great deal said about temperament. I wish they would cut short the word and say, 'There is a great deal in temper.' But as to temperament, I think we are very much mistaken about it. Grace can make us the strongest on the weakest side of our character. Why, what would the Master do with His prodigious strength, if it were not for our weakness? If you are wont to be depressed, the Spirit of God can make you joyous. Alas! how many Christians go out into some scene of earthly enjoyment. They sit down to some novel, or engage themselves about dresses, or go to the theatre ; and they call this the honey of human life, instead of remembering that the kingdom of God is not meat and drink. Thank God, there is enough in the boundless sufficiency of the Spirit of the living God.

Those who were gathered together on the day of Pentecost, were believers who had labored successfully for Christ, and yet there was an advanced experience there that they became real partakers of. Well, but do you mean that we are to have another Pentecost? Dispensationally, no; experimentally, yes ; and no dozen of us could go aside and wait before God for the increase of the power of the Spirit, that we would not realize it. It is on this ground that I never care for people praying for the outpouring of the Holy Spirit, as though they thought of the Holy Spirit being in heaven to be communicated in answer to prayer. Never think of the Spirit of God as away from you ; He dwells within you, and He is to dwell with you forever. An absent Spirit, an absent Father, an absent Christ, is not the teaching of this book : " If any man love Me, him will My Father love, and we will come to him and make our abode with him."

I hear people talk about approaching the Lord. I dare not approach. The Lord made me nigh when I was first converted. I had then liberty to enter within the veil by the precious blood of Jesus, but I have never had any liberty from my Father since then to go out forever. If I ever go out, it is in violation of His will. I beseech you, never allow the thought of distance to find a lodgment in your hearts.

And now I ask you to notice again, the Spirit is shown as of fire. The figure is very beautiful, because you know how naturally cold we are. I say this to you, because I want you to know that you really have no native power. You know what a cold room is in winter time. By your warming arrangements here, the illustration would not do, but it would in England. I have caught a great deal of cold in the latter part of October, and in November, when I have been taken into drawing rooms. I would rather go into the kitchen. It is so nice and warm there, and the drawing rooms are so cold. And so with some Christians ; they are awfully cold. Their big houses do not make them warm. The fact that they have prospered, or that their husbands have occupied high official positions, does not make them warm. They have missed the baptism of fire, and they are cold and must be cold.

5*

"Like as of fire;" so expansive. Oh! the genial warmth.

And here a word of kindly sympathy. Do I say some things that pain you? Am I finding out the weak place? Would you, Christian sister, — would you say to me if we were alone, 'Dear Mr. Varley, my life does sadly break down at home.' I know many who say that to me. My dear friend, I tell you, there is no cure for it until you just get firm hold of this precious truth, the baptism of the Spirit of God in power. Now do not let your coldness hinder you. Suppose that in a fortnight's time, the weather having turned very cold, some friend of yours should come to your house at night and knock at the door, and when the door is opened he refuses to come in. The servant tells you this, and you come out to the door yourself, and you say, 'Oh! pray come in; it is so cold out there.' But he says, 'I can't come in yet.' 'But why can't you come in?" Why, you would make the coldness an additional reason for his coming in. There are thousands of Christians just so cold, and in that darkened condition of the understanding, which I think the devil himself is in; they say, 'I can't come in until I am warm.' I think the precious words of Hart might apply here: "If you tarry till you're better, you will never come at all."

Not only fire, but listen, that "mighty wind." I went when a boy to Australia — I remember the fine old ship that we started in — and when we reached the tropics we were becalmed. It is even now a matter of memory. One day we lowered the boats, and as though the great Atlantic Ocean was a sea of glass, a number of us rowed round the vessel — not one breath of wind — and there she swayed to and fro and her big sails flapped on the masts. Often have I, leaning over the taffrail of the vessel, watched when the sun went down, to see if there were any chance of wind, and the eye would detect in the distance just a little ripple, and in half an hour's time the breeze would overtake us, and soon after we would see those big sails no longer flapping, the ship no longer a lifeless log upon the water, but as though influenced with the energy of vital force, she darted like a bird through the waters, every stitch of canvas filled.

Ah! this is what we want. I have no native energy to move me forwards toward home,—none whatever. I have no native power to help me to preach. Christ says, "Without Me ye can do nothing." God help me with an intense apprehension of this truth. I will throw myself at His feet and say, 'Lord, I will never attempt to do anything. Let me work by Thy power.' As the Psalmist puts it in the forty-fifth Psalm, "My heart is inditing a good matter." The marginal reading is, "It is bubbling up." You have seen the flame beneath a cauldron making the water or other fluid in it boil— what a commotion there is on the surface and pervading it all — that is the way I long to preach the Gospel. · I appeal to my brethren, the ministers of the Gospel, this afternoon, Is it not true, as I confess for myself, that we would rather break stones in the streets than preach the Gospel of Christ

without the baptism of fire. O God! I ask Thee
to forgive me, that I have ever received inspiration
from a crowded audience instead of by the baptism
of the Spirit. Let us remember the Saviour's
pledge, "Lo, I am with you always," and let our
power be not only as we sing with Lynch, in the
Hymn on the Spirit:

> " Mighty Spirit dwell with me,
> I myself would mighty be ;
> Mighty so as to prevail
> Where unaided man must fail ;
> Aided by a mighty hope,
> Pressing on and bearing up—"

but at the same time,

> " Gentle Spirit, dwell with me,
> I myself would gentle be."

Oh! let the tenderness of the Spirit make us like
nurses, or as Paul puts it, as an affectionate mother
over her children. These are some of the precious
blessings that come to us by the gift of the Spirit.
I venture to think that the different sections of the
Church have yet to learn what it is, by that Spirit
to be baptized into one body. I believe that unity
consists not in ecclesiastical systems. I believe
that it is by our recognition by the power of the
Spirit, of the oneness that is ours in Christ Jesus
the Lord. Names have small power to divide.
There is a name ; there is a love that amazes one.
It is the love of Christ ; it is the power of the
Spirit ; it is the name of Jesus. Many things will
harmonize when this is right. O yes, I am sure of

that. I never felt disposed to speak unkindly of
those Christians who differ from me. I am sometimes, for example, with those who think a great
deal of what we call High Church. Now I venture
to say, with great thoughtfulness, that those who
have represented the evangelical section of the
Church, are not a little to blame for their views.

You must bear with me. We have loved and
honored friends in the old country who have been
wise and yet injudicious. I will tell you what they
have said. They have said, " O, give us very plain
buildings ; we do not care for anything ornate.
Give us a plain surplice or gown, as the case may
be. Give us the Prayer Book ; give us the people.
That's all we want." They were right enough in
this, but many a dear brother who has held the
theory of evangelical truth has not life enough.
How cold he has been! how mechanical his service!
how he has lacked the baptism of fire! A dear
fellow, when some of his brethren have come in
and said, "Is this the best representation of the
Gospel we can have," has gone off to an extreme.
I am not surprised at it, and I feel that I would
just as tenderly encompass in the arms of my love
brethren who hold these extreme opinions, as some
others, because I am persuaded that when the High
and the Low get hold of this precious truth of the
power of the Spirit of God, the little things — and
how little they are when you come to it — will
vanish.

I could not understand a man who possessed the
baptism of the Spirit, turning his back to his

congregation and manipulating at some altar. No,
if the soul was filled with the love of Christ, and
possessed by the Holy Spirit of God, he could not
be mechanical, but would say, "Give me the book,
the living power of the Spirit, and if you please, the
open street, four bare walls, what you like ; I have
all I need ; I have the baptism of the Spirit of
God." Oh, brethren, there are hundreds of things
that separate us in this way. "Seeing ye have
purified your souls in obeying the truth through the
Spirit unto unfeigned love of the brethren, see that
ye love one another with a pure heart fervently."
O God, in Thy mercy make us to be filled with the
Spirit. Let us dare to believe that we are. I do
not mean that you should thoughtlessly say to
every one that meets you, " I am filled with the
Spirit." It is not, perhaps, the wise thing. But
seeing that it is written, "Be ye filled with the
Spirit," in the calm faith of God's children who
have the heritage of Christ, let us believe that we
are filled, nevertheless ; and when the vessel is full
of love and joy and peace and gentleness and goodness and meekness and patience and faith, you will
have a compass for these. You will have a love
that will astonish you, because it is not some of
the poor native flow, but the boundless love of the
great Spirit of God.

O Spirit of might and power ! come into us, rest in
us, brood over us, until possessing our whole being,
we may show what God can do with very poor
vessels that are surrendered to Him. Some one
of you says, "Ah, sir, that is just it, a poor vessel."

Well, what of that? what if you are a poor, cracked vessel, letting out the blessing which you receive? I admit that you and I are poor, cracked vessels, letting out that which we receive; but supposing this were a glass, and this a tap, and supposing that I turn the tap, don't you think that if there is a bountiful supply behind, it will keep the vessel full? But the glass may leak.   Yes, but the fountain will keep it full.   Be not discouraged; these wonderful blessings are ours, not because we are worthy, but because Christ loves us.   Christ loves us! we love also.   O Jesus! partakers of Thy endless life, let us know what it is to reproduce that beautiful life over again for Thy glory.   Spirit of God, strengthen us with might in the inner man.   AMEN.

THE

BREAD OF LIFE.

———◦◦;◦;◦◦———

EXODUS XVI. 35.

AND THE CHILDREN OF ISRAEL DID EAT MANNA FORTY YEARS,
UNTIL THEY CAME TO A LAND INHABITED: THEY DID EAT
MANNA, UNTIL THEY CAME UNTO THE BORDERS OF THE LAND
OF CANAAN.

IN more than one address I have endeavored to
point out how fully the Old Testament makes
known the Lord Jesus Christ, and perhaps in
no part does the excellency of Jesus Christ come
out more vividly, than in this beautiful type of the
manna. He himself has given His introduction
to my theme, very distinctly identifying Himself
as the true manna which came down from heaven,
of the which, if a man eat, he shall live forever.
The condition of Israel was such that they must
be supplied by the living God or die. The wilderness could not supply them with food, and since
their unbelief had shut them out of the land flowing with milk and honey; since God had judicially

separated them by His oath, swearing in His wrath that they should not enter into His rest, (and, as you know, that whole generation died, save only Caleb the son of Jephunneh, and Joshua the son of Nun, and the children under twenty years of age, when the oath went forth,) — I pray you observe how this provision was entirely of God's mercy. I should like to identify my theme with the chapter, so that whenever you read it again, the thoughts I express may come to your minds.

Note first, that the manna was provided by God in the dark night of their human need. How precious is the thought thus suggested. When man was lying in the hopelessness of sin, the Eternal God Himself brought in His own wonderful provision. There, upon the ground, the manna lies. I love to think how near it is, and that the Lord Jesus Christ has come to our necessities. "Who shall ascend into heaven, that is to bring Christ down from above, or who shall descend into the deep, that is to bring Christ again from the dead, for the word is nigh thee." Oh that I could take you outside the tents of Israel, and show you there that manna which God so bountifully showered around. There it is, and I would here point out to you the responsibility which rests upon us. Either the manna must be taken up by us or we must tread upon it,—one thing or the other. It must be taken up or trodden down. It lies there in its minute form,—small as coriander seed,— like the hoar-frost on the ground. So abundant has our God made the provision of salvation, that there is not one soul in this house to-night who need leave it unsaved. "He that believeth on Him is not condemned; but he that believeth not is condemned already, because he hath not believed in the name of the only begotten Son of God."

And remember how adapted to the need of the Israelite was this manna, and how beautifully adapted is Jesus Christ, as the bread of life, to every one of us. Still men are idly speculating upon the Lord Jesus as a bundle of doctrines, of difficult theories. But I would ask you to remember how the eternal God has made Him to be the bread which cometh down from Heaven. He cannot bear that you should die; it is the bread which sustains; it is Christ which is the life. He that hath the Son hath life, for as Jesus so sweetly says: 'I am the bread from Heaven, of which if a man eat he shall live forever.' I pray that your minds may be disabused in this beautiful figure, of all the difficulties which may suggest themselves to you about the reception of Christ. Remember that Christ is bread to the soul. He scatters the harvest-field of the world with His presence, and bids you eat. There is not a loaf that finds its way on to your table but it speaks of Jesus to you. It whispers, "I am the bread which came down from Heaven." The hunger of the soul must be appeased. There is a sphere in which you cannot find even the temporary rest which man has now. The rich man, when he passed away into the other world, lifted up his

eyes, being in torment, and asked that Lazarus
might be sent to cool his parched tongue. And
there is an absence of the bread which satisfies,—
an absence which I pray God you and I may never
know, for the time will come when God shall remove this wondrous provision.

Again, observe that although the manna was
given in the dark night of their necessity, it needed
the incoming dawn in order to its discovery. I
am rejoiced that that morning has dawned on the
world's history. The light has come ; as it is
written, " Unto you that fear My name shall the
Sun of righteousness arise with healing in His
wings." Yes, my friends, from your unbelief I call
you, from that dread valley into which many of you
perhaps may be settling : you say, ' I am almost
in despair, for there was a time in my history when
I looked for Christ and when He spoke to me, but
I rejected Him and put away the overtures of His
love.' I charge you remember, that there need
be no hesitation, for the light has come. " I am
come," says Christ, " a light into the world." " He
that followeth me shall not walk in darkness but
shall have the light of life."

Along with the morning light came mists ; there
may be some of you here on whom the light has
come so gradually, that as yet there is a mist on
the face of the condition of your mind. You
are something like the poor man in the Gospel,
of whom it is recorded that he saw men as trees
walking. I have often thought of the beauty of
that simile. The soul seeking for Christ in his

own strength is just like that. He does not know exactly what it is to be saved; there is a dim mist before him, and he does not know what eternal life is. You ask him whether he is whiter than snow; you ask him whether he discerns the difference between salvation by the work of Christ and the imperfect work of the Spirit—he does not know; and there may be some Christians who have never yet seen the difference between the work of Christ and the unfinished work of the Spirit.

I charge you remember this, that you are not saved by the work of the Spirit of God in you, but you are saved by the work of Christ for you. That work of Christ is over; it is completed. You cannot add anything to it. Oh, believe and live. If you were to ask me how I feel as touching the work of Christ for me I should say: Absolutely finished; finished, every jot. If you ask me about the work of the Spirit in me,—I say it thoughtfully,—I never felt it so incomplete as to-night. Oh, that Spirit of God leads us on, and, as we get nearer home, the discovery of that which is before us leads us to cry out with the Apostle: "Not as though I had already attained, either were already perfect: but I follow after, if that I may apprehend that for which also I am apprehended of Christ Jesus. * * * But this one thing I do, forgetting those things which are behind, and reaching forth unto those things which are before, I press toward the mark for the prize of the high calling of God in Christ Jesus." Yes, brethren, again let me point out to you by the light of the rising sun

the essential difference between the finished work
of Christ by which you are saved, and the unfinished work of the Spirit of God, developing the
Christian life in you to-day, and which work is to
go on until the latest hour of your life here upon
the earth.

And now, notice, "when the sun was up,"—they
saw it by the light of the rising sun. The sun for
us is Christ, for He is risen again for our justification, and we can see clearly now that the bread of
God, the life of God, is not something we are in
ourselves, but it is that we receive from Him.
You know how much controversy has raged in
the Church for centuries past about that expression in the sixth of John, where the Lord speaks
about the importance of our eating of His flesh
and drinking His blood ; and the Church of Rome
has gone off into the broad materialistic idea of
transubstantiation, whereby they tell you the flour,
or the bread, and the wine, become the actual
and real body and blood of the Lord Jesus. And
then there is the Ritualist, who gives you a
modified but still very untrue view of the same
doctrine.

Dear friends, let your faith simply perceive this,
that whoever truly receives the body and blood so
represented, is the real Christian, the vital man ;
that you must receive His being into yours by
faith, — mark what I say, — His being with yours,
that is what Christianity is ; it is Christ received.
Let me say to you that Christianity is the reception by faith of God's Christ into your inmost

6

being, until the veins of your spiritual nature are
filled with the veritable blood, the life ; for the life
is in the blood.   It is the actual reception by you
of God's Christ, or, as one has beautifully expressed it, the Lord Jesus descending from the
divine nature to the human, in order that He
might raise the human to the divine, and you and
I, through participation in God's Christ, have partaken of that which makes us one with Him in
dignity of character, in continuity of life, in glorious destiny, "for He is not ashamed to call us
brethren." He says, "Go to my brethren, and say
unto them, I ascend unto my Father and your
Father, and to my God and your God."

However stupendous that thought may be, yet
is it true, oh blessed Christ, that Thou didst
come, — the true bread from heaven, — that we,
receiving Thee, can never die.   Christianity, then,
is not a system of morals, but spiritual life received from Christ, — a participation in the bread
sent down from heaven.   Once again, I want you
to notice the position of the manna ; here it is on
the ground.   I think if this platform upon which
I stand were covered with manna, and it lay there
like coriander seed, it would be the height of folly
for me to attempt to pick it up while in a standing posture.   I could gather it up best by getting
down on my knees.   There is here a thought,
which I pray may abide with you forever.

You remember the woman of Canaan, to whom
the Saviour said, "It is not meet to take the
children's bread and to cast it unto the dogs."

The idea that you, a poor worm of the earth, should eat angels' food! To think that you should become a partaker of the divine nature! to think that you a poor creature, with an uncertain life of thirty, fifty, or seventy years, should be elevated unto participation of the divine! And when Christ tried her faith by saying unto her, "It is not meet to take the children's bread and to cast it unto the dogs," she answered, "Yes, Lord: yet the dogs under the table eat of the children's crumbs." Oh for this same spirit among you all, that every soul here would get down under the table, would get down on his knees, and not think he is patronizing Christ, but receive Him, the Bread of Life, for famishing men.

I would to God that that scene could be enacted here which was enacted by the lepers of old, when the famine was so sore. They said, "If we go into the city it is death, and if we go into the camp it is death." But necessity compelled them to go into the camp, not to die, but to find abundance of provision: and I would that every unconverted soul should come into this condition of sheer necessity. I would to God that you should hear the Master say, in the secret despair which enwraps you, "He that cometh to Me I will in no wise cast out."

Down, then, upon your knees, for the manna lies thick upon the ground. It is there for the old and infirm who will pick it up; it is there, the youth may find it; it is there, the maiden may eat it; it is there, the man in the prime of his days shall eat it, and eating it he shall live forever. *Forever,* is the word.

> "Oh, that glorious word, Forever,
> Yes, *forever* is the word:
> Nothing shall the ransomed sever,
> Naught divide them from their Lord."

They have eaten the bread, they have participated in the life, which if a man once receive, he can never die.   Not only do we want the humility which brings us there, but do you see how God's dignity and our humility meet, as it were.   When we get down into the dust He comes and lifts us up.   He lifts the beggar from the dunghill and sets him among princes.

I ask you to notice another very interesting thought.   They all gathered this manna.   Some gathered more, some less.   How beautiful it is. It is no distressingly hard thing to eat.   It never interferes with the digestion of the smallest child, and it is adapted to the physical nature of the strongest man.   And oh, the adaptation of the Lord Jesus to every one who seeks after spiritual food.   Many get into physical sickness by partaking too freely of that which is most pleasant to the taste.   Do you remember the account given in Exodus of the table of shew bread? on the table which was kept in the holy place of the tabernacle, every Sabbath morning twelve fresh baked loaves were placed before the Lord.   These twelve loaves were made of fine flour, the material was not to be changed, fresh kneaded and fresh baked, and the twelve loaves placed on the table by the High

Priest every returning Sabbath morning. Now it was not a question of what was pleasing to the worshipers, it was a question of what was acceptable to God; and I venture to say the preacher who says, "Will this be acceptable to my people?" is not preaching the gospel of Christ.

While chatting with a Church of England clergyman, not long since, he said to me, " My dear sir, I should be so glad if you could just help me a little. I am a clergyman, and I want to know something about the secret of the power which you seem to possess, for evidently God is with you; and I want to know how my usefulness may be increased." In the course of our conversation he told me that he wrote out his sermons, — I have no objection to this, for it is desirable that what a man has to say on such an important theme should be well studied, — and that he read and re-read them, and if there were any thing which would offend any of the congregation he expunged it. " Oh, sir," I said, " that is enough to make your preaching a failure. My dear friend you must declare the *whole* word of God."

I pray you see that the appetite for Christ is formed before the time comes when there will be no opportunity of embracing this glorious life. Oh, thou blessed One, beget the appetite in many souls. Oh that we might hear the cry, " My soul thirsteth for God," or say, like Jeremiah, " I found thy word and did eat it, and its fruit was sweet unto my taste." See to it, that day by day you be satisfied with Christ.

I do not know whether I ever stated here, that in this Bible of mine, at the end, there is a list of the titles of Jesus Christ. They number three hundred and sixty-seven, — one for every day in the year, and two beyond. Oh, the wondrous fullness there is in Christ. Tell me, brother, do you want a Saviour? He is that. Do you want a Redeemer? He is that. Do you want the Shepherd? He is that. Do you want Love? He is that. Do you want a Keeper? He is that. Do you want the Bread of Life? He is that. Do you want the Rock? Do you want the Water out of it? Do you want the Honey? Do you want the Vine? It is all gathered up in one great fullness, pouring out its eternal plenitude for the sins of men. Go, scatter that manna. Fathers, scatter it for your children; husbands, for your wives, and wives for your husbands. Shake the bread of God until, out of the seed basket, every servant, employee, and friend, shall be brought in contact with the Bread of Life. The abundance that is there! There it lies; and there it must be trodden upon, or it must be gathered up. Send out the children to gather it. It is adapted for the tiniest years; it is adapted for the oldest man; and there it lies, on the face of the camp, given in the dark night; but the night passed, the rising sun discovers its whereabouts. Do pick it up, and continue eating and live.

Brethren, I call you to the feast, — the feast which God has so richly provided; and I pray you remember the figure, it is bread; it is adapted to our common needs. One of your American preachers has said that Christianity is indeed the Bread of Life, but says he, " Alas, alas, how many Christians there are who do not seem to understand the appropriateness of this figure! When I was a boy I used to get a loaf and would keep trimming slices off, around and around ; and so I went through my boyhood to manhood, eating constantly of the bread which nourisheth ; and so my stature increased. It was growth by taking hold of the bread ; but, alas, many, many Christians make cake of it, and they put it away in the cupboard, and then, if they do ever bring it out, hand it around on china plates, as much as to say to friends, the less of it you eat the better." There is a great deal of truth in his quaint, sarcastic reproof.

I beg of you take this Bread and eat it, and eating it you shall live forever. I beseech you let the Lord Jesus Christ fill the heaven of your soul, and cry out, in the language of the Scriptures, " Thanks be unto God for His unspeakable gift." Eat this Bread, take it into your inmost being, and you shall experience the truth of what the Psalmist says : " Thy word have I hid in my heart, that I should not sin against Thee." And let me beg of you to get up early in the morning and eat of this manna. Early in the morning they went out to find it. We read that when the sun arose the manna was spoiled. If you let the early hours of the morning pass by, if you do not unlock the day, as it were, with God, I have observed there

is but little chance of redeeming it at noon-time.
No, this manna must be taken in the morning, and
when by this diligent gathering of Christ your
vessel runs over, go and share it with those you
meet. Go, strong, vigorous man, and share it at
the bedside of your sick one. Go, father, and
speak of it to thy child. Go, wife, and speak of it
to thy husband.

There is One yonder, into whose hands the
government of the eternal ages is delegated, and
with whom centuries of men are to reign. I venture to believe that the world is far nearer the
final issue than we think for. I look back upon
the great downfalls of the earth's mightiest powers, covered with commercial prosperity, — Rome
and its splendor have decayed, Greece has gone,
and in later history, France has been shaken, and
how I tremble for England. England! exalted to
the heavens; the first nation which has ripened
to her noon-day life side by side with her open
Bible, — the highest privilege a nation has ever
known, — I fear that Christ shall say of her, as
He said of Capernaum of old, ' O, thou England,
exalted to heaven with privileges, thou art cast
down to hell.' I cannot shut my eyes to the
burden of the testimony of that book, that this
dispensation closes with solemn, overwhelming
judgment. If I could I would, but I dare not;
the mass of testimony by Christ is so overwhelming. And I charge you, brethren, see to it that
your wives, your children, your husbands, your
fathers, your mothers, your brothers, your sisters,

have an appetite for Christ. The appetite for gold cannot live longer. The appetite for commerce has no place. The lusts, the desires, the passions, have no place there ; but God.

Let that part of your being which shall live on, and on, in the splendor of that life which Christ imparts, let that be impregnated with Christ. Oh, brothers, sisters, children, young men and maidens, I plead with you, with all the energy of which my soul is capable, let not this manna, this Christ, come down from heaven,—and yet ask, like the Jews, a sign, while the bread is before you. Do not run away after petty side issues. I remember a young lady saying to me, as we were traveling together from London, " Oh, Mr. Varley, I am so anxious to be in the true Church." I said to her, " My sister, let me read to you ; " and, taking my Bible from my pocket, I read to her these words: " While he yet talked to the people, behold, his mother and his brethren stood without, desiring to speak with him. Then one said unto him, Behold, thy mother and thy brethren stand without, desiring to speak with thee. But he answered and said unto him that told him, Who is my mother? and who are my brethren? And he stretched forth his hand toward his disciples, and said, Behold my mother and my brethren! For whosoever shall do the will of my Father which is in heaven, the same is my brother, and sister, and mother."

Where is salvation? In the Church of Rome? Yes ; in every man is salvation in whose heart

Christ dwells. Where is salvation — in the Church of England? Yes; in every heart where Christ dwells. Where is Christ, and where is Christianity? In the Wesleyan Church? Yes; in just so many whose hearts enshrine Christ, and no more. Where is Christianity? Among the Presbyterians or the Baptists? Yes; if Christ is in the heart, but if not, their systems are a delusion and a snare, and may be to them eternal loss; for there is many a man whose name is transcribed upon the register of the Church, who knows nothing about the life of Christ. There is a name — the name of Jesus — and to that common centre, by the impulse of the Spirit of God, men gravitate from every Church. You cannot divide them, for they are one.

The Church of God is not a little band, kept together by the *ipse dixit* of some Church or body of bishops. Over China, India, Africa, Australia, Europe, and America, broods the mighty Spirit of God, and beneath His sheltering wing couches the entire Church of God, of every name, of every clime, of every color, for there shall be gathered from every nation, kindred, people and tongue, a numberless company who have fed upon God's life, — men and women to whom Christ is precious. Oh, brethren, I give you my closing words in the Master's name: Are you feeding upon Christ's precious truth?

We sat, some of us, at the table of the Lord, and, as I tasted the bread and as the wine passed these lips, I thanked God for His Christ, that had passed into the tissue and fibre of this being, and permeated it by His glorious life. "This is the bread, of which if a man eat he shall live forever." Matchless life! Glorious bread! O, Thou blessed God, to have opened Thy hands and scattered this eternal bread amongst the dying sons of men. The day is coming when we shall know, as we cannot know now, the glory of this life; for now we see darkly, as through a glass, but then face to face. Now we know in part; now abideth faith, hope and love; but when the end shall have come, and you and I shall shake off the tabernacle of clay which keeps us here, we shall know then what is meant by living upon Christ.

Would to God that every merchant, every student, every clerk, would give Christ the front; that every politician would give Christ the front; for this is the sum total: "I am Alpha and Omega, the beginning and the end, the first and the last." Blessed Christ! Blessed Bread! May my poor description of Thee entice hundreds to come out of their tent, and on their knees and in their souls, by the light of truth, pick up and eat that manna, and no longer feed upon the husks which the swine eat. I know that the devil has food for you. I know that there is a counterfeit of the wheat in the tares. I know it; but in Christ's name I beseech you see to it that no false Christ keeps you from Christ. I leave these solemn weighty appeals which should tell upon your destiny forever: I leave them in the hand of the Eternal God, who has said, "My word shall not return unto Me void. For as the rain cometh down, and the snow from heaven, and returneth not thither, but watereth the earth, and maketh it bring forth and bud, that it may give seed to the sower, and bread to the eater: so shall My word be that goeth forth out of My mouth."

NICODEMUS.

THIS evening I propose to address* you from thoughts contained in the third chapter of the Gospel of John, as touching the interview between Nicodemus and the Great Master; and I shall endeavor to make my remarks, as far as I possibly can, subserve the object of this meeting in the interest of young men. "There was a man of the Pharisees, named Nicodemus, a ruler of the Jews: The same came to Jesus by night, and said unto Him, Rabbi, we know that Thou art a teacher come from God: for no man can do these miracles that Thou doest, except God be with Him." What an important time has come in the history of a man, when his desire after a knowledge of the Lord Jesus Christ leads him to the Master Himself. Such a time as this had come to Nicodemus, and such a time I trust has come to many of you who are found

---

* This Address was delivered by Mr. Varley at the Seventh Anniversary Meeting of the Hamilton Young Men's Christian Association, held in the Centenary Church, Hamilton, Canada, on the evening of Friday, December 4, 1874.

in this house to-night. I want you now to notice
how the Lord Jesus deals with Nicodemus. "Jesus
answered and said unto him, Verily, verily, I say
unto thee, except a man be born again, he cannot
see the kingdom of God. Nicodemus saith unto
Him, How can a man be born when he is old? can
he enter the second time into his mother's womb,
and be born? Jesus answered, Verily, verily, I say
unto thee, except a man be born of water and of
the Spirit, he cannot enter into the kingdom of
God."

You will observe in these words, that there is
apparently no connection between the question
which is put by Nicodemus, and the answer given
by the Lord. The reason of this I think is obvious.
Nicodemus wanted Christ to do what many men in
our day want Him to do. He wanted Christ to
educate before converting ; and I assure you, my
friends, that the Master will never do that. He
will bear with you ; He will be full of tenderness,
and full of long suffering and gentleness ; but as
surely as I am speaking to you to-night, the Master
will deal with you in this peremptory way, as suddenly as He did with Nicodemus : " Verily, verily,
I say unto thee, except a man be *born again*, he
cannot see the kingdom of God." The reason of
this I will try and illustrate to you. What would
you think of me were I to go to a teacher of eti-
quette, and say to him : " Sir, I understand you are
schooled in the laws of Court, and you teach kings
and nobles how to demean themselves in the high
places of the land : I want you to teach me how to

wear a crown; how to hold with becoming dignity a levee." "But pardon me," is the reply, "are you a king? "No." "You have no expectancy of the crown?" "Not the least." "And you want me to educate you, do you!" Would not the absurdity of the thing justify his derisive laugh, as he turns and leaves you? And yet, that is what thousands of men are wanting. They are wanting Jesus Christ to educate a lifeless being; they are wanting Him to dress up that which God rejects. "Verily, verily, I say unto thee, except a man be born again," there is no life to develop, there is not a *man* to teach or educate. There is not a soul listening to my voice who was born into the world with spiritual life; it is not ours by hereditary right, by infant or adult baptism, by sprinkling or immersion. "He that *hath the Son hath life*," but he that hath not the Son of God, though he may be the mightiest intellect in the earth, though he may be the wisest of politicians, and have the largest perception of mundane affairs, though he may be as eloquent as Demosthenes, yet if he has not Christ, he is destitute of life.

The Master's words generally strike home at once, and, by His sharp and keenly directed arrow, He has hit the centre of Nicodemus's mind. Nicodemus has not misunderstood Him. Nicodemus said unto Him: "How can a man be born when he is old? can he enter the second time into his mother's womb and be born?" Jesus answered, "Verily, verily, I say unto thee, except a man be born of water and of the Spirit, he cannot enter into the kingdom of God. That which is born of the flesh is flesh ; and that which is born of the Spirit is spirit." Mark the sharp division here: "that which is born of the flesh is flesh," and, dear friends, you may do with it what you like—you may develop it, you may educate it, you may restrain it, you may circumcise it, you may teach it to pray, you may baptize it, you may bring it to the holy table of the Lord, you may put its name on the Church's book, —and when you have done all, it will remain flesh still. That which is born of the flesh remains flesh still, you can never alter it, and God has not designed its alteration. He has designed its judgment, He has designed its putting away, He has designed its rejection ; and the man who is in the Spirit can say, "Thank God, I am not in the flesh, but in the Spirit."

Now notice again, "born of water and of the Spirit." Do you remember how, when the angel came to Mary, he said to her, " The power of the Highest shall overshadow thee : therefore also that holy thing which shall be born of thee shall be called the Son of God." Unless the Divine Spirit brood over you, and sow the seed of incorruptible truth in your heart, and that truth germinate there, you will never know what it is to be born again, nor enabled to say in the language of Peter, ' As a new born babe, I desire the sincere milk of the word that I may grow thereby.' The ministry of the Spirit of God alone can accomplish this, and therefore, when Nicodemus asks Jesus, listen to what He says : "The wind bloweth where it listeth,

and thou hearest the sound thereof, but canst not
tell whence it cometh, and whither it goeth: so is
every one that is born of the Spirit." The wind!
There is not a child here but has felt its gentle play
upon its face; there is not one of us who has not
watched its rustle among the million leaves of the
forest, sometimes delicate as a fairy's wand; but
mark again its tempestuous power, as we see it
swaying the mighty oak and driving the rolling
waves of yonder Atlantic. And again, we have
seen it swelling the hurricane and sweeping away
with its tempestuous power aught which stands in
its path. Who ever saw the source of the wind?
You say it is coming from the northeast, but where
is the corner from whence it came? It is passing
us at the rate of forty or more miles an hour, and
as you watch the movement of yon fleeting cloud,
so it is with every one who is born of the Spirit.
Oh! what can your believer in " Baptismal Regeneration " say, by the side of such a doctrine as that?
What can your scientific theorist say, if he bend
not to the teaching of Christ. It is a constant
enigma that his understanding can never solve; so
simple, and yet so marvellous. Blessed be God,
that that Divine Spirit is to-night brooding over
every soul in this house. There is not one here
to-night a stranger to the Spirit's power. He is
carrying on His ministrations now. ' When He,
the Spirit of Truth, is come, He shall reprove
the world of sin." You cannot help thus being
reproved. You cannot get away from it; it is
from the earthly to the sensual, and from the sen-

sual to the devilish. You cannot stop at the earthly; you cannot stop at the sensual. Just as certainly as the waters of yonder lake find their way to the mighty Atlantic, the earthly empties into the sensual, and the sensual into the devilish. The other way, the earthly has an upward tendency! from the earthly to the spiritual, and from the spiritual to the heavenly—that is God's plan—right up to the throne.

And now once again note, "Born of water." Well, and what do you think that is? The Lord Jesus said to the woman of Samaria at the well, "If thou knewest the gift of God, and who it is that saith to thee, Give me to drink; thou wouldest have asked of Him, and He would have given thee living water." Now, I believe the water spoken of by Christ is the Word; because the Word and the water are often used as synonymous terms. "Wherewithal shall a young man cleanse his way? By taking heed thereto according to Thy Word;" and then take that wonderful passage in the fifth of Ephesians: "As Christ also loved the church, and gave Himself for it; that He might sanctify and cleanse it with the washing of water by the Word." A poor skeptic in London came to me not long ago, and said, "I have been an infidel lecturer, Mr. Varley, for years; what can such a sinner as I do?" I said, "My dear friend, let me bring to you the water of purity, and I shall pour it into your heart until it shall sluice out from it the vile thoughts which have been lodging and corroding there for years." It is the water of the

Word, and if any man shall receive that water into his heart, I tell you, it shall cleanse the heart of the defilement which has been collecting there for years. " Except a man be born of water," or as the apostle Peter says—" Not of corruptible seed, but of incorruptible, by the word of God, which liveth and abideth for ever."

I ask you, then, have you become possessed of that new life which Jesus came to impart to the sons of men ? Have you drank of that water ? Has that water put out the fever fires of sin, which were burning in your breast ? Oh ! I trust so. Young men, I beseech you remember that the life which Jesus has brought is a life of dignity ; it is a life of calmness ; it is a life of power ; it is a life which will help you to put your foot upon the neck of passion ; it is a life that, when understood, shall make it difficult to do wrong and easy to do right ; it is a life which, when you possess it, you shall find has in it a charm and fascination ; it is a life worthy of Jesus Christ to bring. Oh ! the excellency of it. " Marvel not that I said unto thee, Ye must be born again." Some of us, who have known this life for years, can testify of its hold upon our character. We do not speak about holding the Life, but we speak of the Life holding us. " We love Him, because He first loved us." We are not surprised that we love Him with heart and soul and mind and strength, for one of the most essential points in His character is this, that He is LOVE. It is His presence in us that is our joy and song from morning to night ; and as I have said before,

I would, if I could, so spread this power over my life, that I should never think another thought or do another act in mine own strength. I beseech you, let your soul take possession of that new life which God has given, and let us reject the old life, which is condemned and dead.

As Nicodemus listens to His word, Jesus explains to Him : "And as Moses lifted up the serpent in the wilderness, even so must the Son of man be lifted up : that whosoever believeth in Him should not perish, but have eternal life." I quote this passage because of the two "musts." " Ye *must* be born again." " The Son of man *must* be lifted up." I believe these form a kind of conjunction. You must know the new life by looking at Jesus, who said, " I must be lifted up."

> " There is life in a look at the crucified One ;
> There is life at this moment for thee ;
> Then look, sinner, look unto Him and be saved,
> Unto Him who was nailed to the tree."

Just as surely as you *believe* that Jesus died for you, you are *dead* to sin. Once crucified, then always dead. I beseech you, brethren, remember that the life which Christ has brought is to be our charm, our possession, and our glory *forever ;* and in that body that you and I shall soon possess, incorruptible and undefiled, which cannot fade, changed by His glorious body, in the inheritance which is waiting to be revealed, reserved in heaven for us, we shall understand what it is to be clothed upon with this glorious life in Him. Oh! Christian young men, I commend this to you, and as you go out amongst

those who come to your city, keep this to the front.
I tell you what is diminishing the power of our
Young Men's Christian Associations greatly, is a
sort of mongrel thing, half-spiritual, half-worldly.
Some young men want the billiard table in their
Rooms ; some of them in England want to know
if it is not a wise thing to have beer there ! What
we want in our day is a grand, clear conception
of the manliness and vigor of true Christian life,
not namby-pambyism, or such a caricature of the
Christian man as we find put upon the stage—
some long, gaunt fellow, six feet four inches in
height, with his poor seedy coat buttoned close up
to the neck as if he had no shirt beneath. Poor
fellow, he is the very picture of cant. We hear
men speak of the cant of Christians. I suppose
there is not a particle of cant in their rejection of
Christ ! I am ashamed of Charles Dickens to
think that not a single character of a Christian
man has he written but is a miserable caricature.
As my dear friend Spurgeon once said : " Young
men, be careful that you be manly and natural."

And then, I would like to see you also have a
definite object before you. I believe that one great
curse in the Church is indefiniteness. I believe
that young men ought to ask themselves this question : " Have I got a clear, definite view of what
Christianity is, or am I allowing year after year to
pass by — and precious time is passing — and yet
never thinking seriously of these things ? " Have
you been taken up with smoking, with the cultiva-
tion of some worthless habit or some frivolous

pursuit ? I see so much of this in England, and not a little of it here. I never knew a man yet worth a dollar, who was a dandy. I am not speaking of money, for somehow or other these men do sometimes get hold of money ; but I mean what is *in* the man. I believe there is no development of character that can at all compare with the glorious fullness which the Lord Jesus Christ is prepared to impart. I like that type of character of which John the Baptist was the representative. I do not wonder that the Lord Jesus should say, " Among those that are born of women there is not a greater prophet than John the Baptist." Although he was a rough man and his words tremendously heavy, all Judea was held spell-bound by them, and there was a power about his rugged words which men felt. If there is a type of character I dislike, it is the " Oh yes, Mr. Varley, I quite agree with you " style of man. I do like a man, who, if he differs from you, says so *to* you, and one who can bear and forbear — a man in whom individuality is strongly marked ; not namby-pamby, without backbone— *a man*, that is what I mean. Says one, " An honest man 's the noblest work of God." I tell you, we might improve on that. A converted man — a man in whom Christ dwells — is the noblest work of God.

Now, dear brethren, I am sure if you will carry out these thoughts of mine to-night, the world will not let you alone. I know there will be people studying you, and those who do not like your spirituality will put it down to hypocrisy. " Never

you mind," do you keep straight on. I got a famous
lesson some time since from a certain man of color,
who used to go with his master to church. His
master would sit down in church, and as was his
wont, would have his note book before him, and
when any good point struck him in the sermon, he
would jot it down, which, by the way, is a very
good practice. Sam, who, no doubt as you know—
because you are nearer him here than we are on
the other side — is apt to be a very imitative individual, and he was so delighted with the idea, that
a few Sundays afterwards he provided himself with
a pencil and book. You should have seen him with
his shining face, bobbing head, note book and
pencil. The preacher saw Sam taking notes, and
was so delighted at his apparent interest, that when
the service was over, he made his way down the
aisle to Sam, and said, " Good morning." " Good
mornin', massa." " I am delighted to see you so
interested in the service." " Very interestin' indeed, massa," replied Sam. " You take notes,
Sam." " Indeed, massa, every gentleman takes
notes." " Would you mind my seeing your notes.
Sam ? " " No, massa, not in de least." Now it so
happened that Sam could not write, and when he
handed his note book to the minister, it was scrib-
bled all over with pencil marks. The minister said,
" Oh, Sam, this is all nonsense." " Oh ! deah yes,
massa, de berry thing I thought when you said it."

Oh ! beloved brethren, do walk through this
earth just a memento of what the grace of Christ

can make you—that brain of yours a place in which
the Lord Jesus Christ shall think. Does that
startle you? Not stronger than the Scripture puts
it. Jesus Christ shall develop the most wonderful
thoughts. I tell you to-night that thousands of
the best thoughts I have ever given utterance to,
never occurred to me until the moment I spoke.
Some may say it is genius. I believe it is Christ in
me. You say, perhaps, it is originality. I would
not lay claim to that, but I would lay claim to the
possession of Christ. Nor does it seem to be an
extraordinary thing that He who fills yonder sun
with light, should fill my brain with every thought I
possess. I see Him clothing the beautiful earth with
flowers, and spangling yonder heaven with stars;
and shall He do naught in the temple of this body?
Away with such thoughts! If your heart be filled
with the love of Christ, you will be no mean exponent of His character. You shall say with Paul,
"For me to live is Christ." Let this be so, and
there shall flow from your life results beautiful to
think of, and you shall glorify the Master in it too.

I shall close just with one thought, which, perhaps, some of you may not have noticed. You
remember upon one occasion, when the work of
John the Baptist was over — what a wonderful
career it was!—nine months, perhaps not more than
eight, did his ministry last; the most popular man
in Judea; thousands listening to his lessons; his
life gathered in that one brief seed-time and harvest; a wonderful life, the burden of it giving
witness for Christ and testimony for Jesus — they

came to Him and said: "Rabbi, he that was with Thee beyond Jordan, to whom thou barest witness, behold, the same baptizeth, and all men come to him." Why do they say this? The most casual thinker will see that it was said to stir up John's envy. 'But a few weeks ago you were the mightiest man in all this region ; you bore witness to One who is called Christ, and now He is baptizing : He has taken the wind out of your sails.' He "to whom thou bearest witness, behold, the same baptizeth, and all men come to Him." Listen to John's reply : ' "A man can receive nothing, except it be given him from heaven. Ye yourselves bear me witness, that I said, I am not the Christ, but that I am sent before Him. He that hath the bride is the bridegroom : but the friend of the bridegroom, which standeth and heareth him, rejoiceth greatly because of the bridegroom's voice." You have come to fill me with envy, but thus " my joy therefore is fulfilled." It is true, I got off the platform, and let the loveliness of my Master be seen. " He must increase, but I must decrease." ' Ah, sirs, is it any wonder that Christ should say, "Among them that are born of women there hath not risen a greater than John the Baptist." Not a rich man, not lettered in the world's learning, not a politician, not a member of Parliament—No ; the sod, wherever it is, which covers that great and holy man's grave, speaks not of his interest in mundane affairs. There lies a man, rough in exterior, whose meat was locusts and wild honey, but who was baptized of the Spirit, and possessed of

7

the life of Christ; he stands now in unsullied
beauty before the shrine of his Master in heaven.
Galilee is gone; Jerusalem is laid in ruins, and the
land trodden down just as Christ said it should be:
but in the sparkling, dazzling eternity is the man
John.   He was willing to decrease here, that he
might stand as a pillar in the temple of God, to go
out no more forever.   God grant that your life may
be like his.

Young men, see to it that you do not get out of
the Royal Line.   I was once visiting the wondrous
cave of Matlock, and as we came up to the station,
I saw an engine emerging from the distant tunnel.
I said to my friends, " Yonder comes our train ; "
but when it reached the platform, we found it was
but a mineral train, carrying coal and iron, and so
it was turned on to the side track.   Why was this
done ?   To make room for yonder engine which is
coming out of the tunnel's mouth, carrying behind
it living freight — carriages filled with men and
women.   I said to my companions, and this would
I say to you, 'Be careful that you do not carry
mere material, for if you do, God will turn you
away.   He will make room for the men and women
who are freighted with living souls.   *On the Main
Line* mind that you keep!'   Not money, but man ;
not pleasure, but the will of God ; not earth, but
heaven!   Write this inscription by the light of that
glorious truth upon your life, and God shall bless
you, and God, even our God, shall welcome you!

CHRIST'S MESSAGE TO PETER.

MARK XVI. 7.

BUT GO YOUR WAY, TELL HIS DISCIPLES AND PETER THAT HE
GOETH BEFORE YOU INTO GALILEE.

YOU are aware that these words were spoken by the angel, and intended to comfort the sorrowing disciples, who were mourning the death of their Lord. I am not now dealing with the general aspect of the text, but the one thought which is suggested by the introduction of the Apostle Peter's name. Why did not Jesus, or the angel who was Christ's servant, say, "Go tell my disciples and John"? Why did he not do that? John rested on the bosom of the Lord. John was most intimate with Jesus, and I suppose, indeed, the only one of the disciples who followed the Master to the Cross.

In the nineteenth chapter of John, twenty-fifth and twenty-sixth verses, you will find these words: "Now there stood by the cross of Jesus His mother, and His mother's sister, Mary the wife

of Cleophas, and Mary Magdalene, * * * and the
disciple standing by, whom He loved." So far
as I know there is no account of the presence of
any other of the disciples; yet you see the Lord
does not send the message to John. Why? I feel
that there is a great and deep reason why, and I
want to talk to you about that reason, in order that,
supposing there should be present any of us who
are conscious of having, like Peter, denied our Lord,
we may get a wonderful restoration. I do not know
that I could desire any thing higher than that you
should leave this house without the shadow of a
cloud between you and the Lord.

Now doubtless it may be familiar to you that the
very last time that Peter had seen the Lord Jesus,
was at the very time that he betrayed Him;—betrayed Him in terrible oaths. Let us look for a
moment at the fourteenth chapter of Mark, sixty-
sixth verse:

"And as Peter was beneath in the palace, there cometh
one of the maids of the high priest: and when she saw Peter
warming himself, she looked upon him, and said, And thou
also wast with Jesus of Nazareth. But he denied, saying, I
know not, neither understand I what thou sayest. And he
went out into the porch; and the cock crew. And a maid
saw him again, and began to say to them that stood by, This
is one of them. And he denied it again. And a little after,
they that stood by said again to Peter, Surely thou art one of
them; for thou art a Galilean, and thy speech agreeth thereto.
But he began to curse and to swear, saying, I know not this
man of whom ye speak. And the second time the cock crew.
And Peter called to mind the word that Jesus said unto him,
Before the cock crow twice, thou shalt deny me thrice. And
when he thought thereon, he wept."

He never saw his loving Master again until after His resurrection : and I want to show you, dear friends, that although Peter had betrayed and denied his Lord, yet the love of the Lord Jesus Christ continued towards Peter, and that is why the angel was commissioned and received the testimony of the Lord Himself : "Go tell My disciples and Peter!" Oh! though we deny Him, it is certain He abideth faithful. How utterly unlike any thing human this is. If it were, the message would have been : " Is this My chiefest follower? Is this the mode of treatment at the hour of My trial and humiliation ? Let it be so ; he is utterly unworthy of My love. I have borne with him month after month, and year after year, but the climax is now reached. Henceforth we are strangers." I think of the agony of Peter's mind. He had no means of ascertaining what the Lord thought about it. Had he gone to the sepulchre he would have seen the lips of the Lord closed in death ; he could not get a word from Him as to what He thought of his denial, and yet in that wonderful love, in that love which passeth the love of the mother for her child, in that love which is changeless, of which the prophet sings, " I have loved thee with an everlasting love," He sends out upon this fair morning of the resurrection—the morning on which the powers of hell had been destroyed forever : 'Go, tell my disciples *and Peter*, that He goeth before you.' Now, beloved friends, let that thought suffice for the suggestion of my theme.

I want, next, to show you that the Lord Jesus

not only went, as His word declared, but that He
really found Peter; and mark, a special messenger
is sent to make Peter acquainted with the fact that
the Lord Jesus Christ has searched him out. Can
we by the testimony of the Scriptures—(for the
longer I am a preacher the longer do I desire to get
into all my testimony, exposition)—find out from
the Word of God whether the Lord Jesus Christ
carried out this, His intention? Now turn with me
to the twenty-fourth chapter of the gospel of Luke,
where there is a verse, (the thirty-third,) which will
throw some light upon the subject: "And they rose
up the same hour, and returned to Jerusalem, and
found the eleven gathered together, and them that
were with them, saying, The Lord is risen indeed,
and hath appeared to Simon." Now mark the word
there, "The Lord is risen indeed, and hath appeared
unto *Simon*."

A still stronger corroboration is found in the
fifteenth chapter of First Corinthians, fifth verse:
"And that He was seen of Cephas, then of the
twelve." Not of the twelve and then of Cephas.
Why this order? For this simple reason: Imagine
the Lord Jesus gathering together into that room
about which we read, Peter, James, John and the
other disciples, all conscious of the fact of the
denial of Peter. They had doubtless some of them
heard the oaths and curses with which he had
denied his Lord. What a mortifying position. It
seems to me if I had been Peter, I could not have
stood in that place. How could I, for the first
time, see my Lord? No; *not the public rebuke*, but

the *private restoration:* that is the order of divine love.

Now let me ask you, is not this in harmony with the Master's own precious way? Perhaps you will say to me, " I had not read in the Word about Jesus Christ having a private interview with Peter." I pointed it out to you, " The Lord is risen indeed and has appeared unto Simon." If you will turn with me to the eighteenth chapter of Matthew, fifteenth verse—I want that this should become an example to us:—" Moreover if thy brother shall trespass against thee, go and tell him his fault between thee and him alone: if he shall hear thee, thou hast gained thy brother. But if he will not hear thee, then take with thee one or two more, that in the mouth of two or three witnesses every word may be established. And if he shall neglect to hear them, tell it unto the church."

Is it not lovely?—and in the example which I have cited to you we have the precious truth of the course pursued by the Lord Jesus Christ Himself. Oh! how I would like, if I could, to have seen the meeting between those two; the loving Master and the penitent Peter!—the Master, with that long suffering sympathy and tenderness, just resting on Peter yonder, and that strange impulsive nature of Peter's, looking at his Lord. O! that wretched, dread spirit of denial that possessed him,—how he loathes himself. I doubt not he wept at the feet of his Lord; I doubt not he poured out again, as he had done before, the sorrow of heart that possessed him. And thus the Lord Jesus has given

to us a striking example of the way in which the
divine love pursues its object. He does not even
suffer the great item and fact of death to alter it.

I call your attention to the love of the Lord Jesus
for Peter, when He called him, when He bore with
his waywardness, after Peter denied Him in the
judgment hall; many waters cannot quench it,
—death has no power to alter it,—and O! the joy
which ought to come to us that the same blessed
Christ is with us now. There is not a phase of
tenderness which attached to Him on earth but
belongs to Him now. Are some of you carrying
up to this point the memory of some great transgression; have you been on your faces weeping
about it? Let this be the day that from henceforth
you weep no more. The Master's love is such that
as you sit here you may have the restoration, even
as Peter had it, while you listen to the voice of His
love, and when you come to your holy communion
season you may take your places with the highest
amongst those who love Him, conscience at rest,
all healed; and having peace under the restoring
power of His love, you will know the blessing of
this scene by having it re-enacted.

Again, let me remind you of this: that the Lord
Jesus has given us an example that we should follow
in His steps. I do not know that anything ever
made me feel more deeply my utter nothingness as
a Christian, than a talk I had a short time ago with
a beloved Christian brother in England. I knew
him well and had a great regard for him. He was
a public man, and like most public men now-a-days,

continually being charged with all kinds of things; and when chatting with him one day, he said to me, "O! my dear brother, I cannot tell you the joy that it is to me to entirely forgive each one. I cannot tell you the intense pleasure I feel in going into the presence of my Father in prayer, and saying, 'O, my Father, do Thou bless these.'" I never felt so small as I did in the presence of that man; and yet it is what the Master tells us: "Pray for them which despitefully use you, * * * that ye may be the children of your Father which is in heaven."

Beloved friends, I tell you there could be no brighter thing happen to us to-day than to be completely submerged in the love of God. Are not all of us conscious of the danger to which we are exposed in our Christian life, coming into contact with those whom we ought to forgive, and do not. You may say, "I am righteously indignant." Very well. Keep it, and you will see that it will corrode your spiritual life. O! the boundless forgiveness of God. What a paradise it would make this land, from one end to the other, if the spirit of divine forgiveness had but its mighty play in the hearts of all God's people.

At the close of the twelfth chapter of First Corinthians, we find the Apostle saying, "But covet earnestly the best gifts, and yet show I unto you a more excellent way." Now those of you who are familiar with Corinthians, well know that the twelfth chapter is taken up with spiritual gifts, and the fourteenth is taken up with the order of worship, the manner in which our assemblies are to be con-

ducted, etc. What is the thirteenth? Do you observe—some of you may smile at what I am going
to say—that the thirteenth comes in between the
twelfth and fourteenth. How very natural it is, but
mark the thirteenth chapter is studded with the
more excellent way; better than the gift and order:
—*the love.* Do not forget it. I know many men
who have the gift, and order, but not the love. I
am sure I have known some Christian men having
for every pound of knowledge only two ounces of
love. I do not mind sitting at a distance and hearing what they have to say—so angular, so precise,
and so much order. I tell you what you want done
with your gift and order. Like gold possessed of
iron, you want to come and put them into the fire
of the thirteenth chapter, and then they will be
workable. You never can work them well until
you do. It is as though God should say to you:
"My dear children, I come to you upon the first
Sabbath of the year, and offer you that grace which,
if you but possess, will enable you to supply every
demand made upon you. You may be misunderstood; fair motives will be judged falsely; you will
come into contact with brethren that you will find
human, and surly, and ignorant, and wanting in
tenderness; but I give to you that of which it is
written; 'it suffereth long and is kind, envieth not,
vaunteth not itself, is not puffed up, doth not be-
have itself unseemly, seeketh not her own, is not
easily provoked, thinketh no evil, rejoiceth not in
iniquity, but rejoiceth in the truth; beareth all things,
believeth all things, hopeth all things, endureth all

things. Prophecies shall fail, tongues shall cease, but love shall never fail.'" O! that each of you may receive more and more of this "excellent way."

Had the Master left Peter alone, what about Pentecost, what about those three thousands of souls gathered by one simple testimony of that restored man? I tell you it were worth a fall to know the restoring love of the Lord Jesus Christ. I say it not to make you careless about sin — God forbid I should — yet I pity the man who has not experienced himself the divine forgiveness. Forbear one another, and forgive one another, even as God for Christ's sake has forgiven us. I fear many of us have not pushed out into the depths of the divine love. It is spoken of in this wise: "That ye, being rooted and grounded in love, may be able to comprehend with all saints what is the breadth, and length, and depth, and height: and to know the love of Christ, which passeth knowledge." It strikes me some of us have been like children playing on the beach of our great Father's love, rather than pushing off on the depths, and lengths, and breadths and heights of it.

Brethren, I believe it is just this we want to make our characters lovely. I believe there is many a man of business who, if he really possessed this, would bring to his Master many other children. I know what business is. I have had some experience in the old country. I know how the markets, and ups and downs of business, hammer a man into hardness. Dear brother Moody says: " They think so little of gold in the world to come, that they make paving stones of it." O! that you and I may realize that there is only one thing that *abides*. "Now abideth faith, hope, love, * * * but the greatest of these is love." And thus may it be throughout all these years. Let us be careful not to utter words of unkindness to others. I pray you bear a word of exhortation here. It seems to me that one of the weaknesses of our Christian life is the disposition and tendency which many Christians possess, to say some unkind thing about their fellow Christians. If you cannot say something that is kind,—very well, then be quiet.

You know that in the tabernacle service there was always a pair of golden snuffers and golden snuff dishes, but no extinguishers. Some Christians seem to me as if they would all the time like to be extinguishing their fellow Christians. We do not want anything of that kind. And mark what I say to you: the snuffers were made of pure gold; not a rusty old pair, worth but two-pence. Some people have got a little idea of snuffing, and they take the impressions of somebody's character, and carry the foul, smoking stuff into some friend's house. I charge you, beloved, beware. In the snuff dish there was a little indentation, about three-fourths of an inch in depth and one inch square, in order that a small quantity of water might always be kept in it. As soon as the light was snuffed the excresence was taken to that water and the offence at once stayed. How full of teaching.

Let us be careful! I do not mean to say that there are not times in which it may be well for you and me in faithful love to speak to others ; but let us so seek to remove the excrescence, that the light of the brother or sister may shine more brightly. Let us put away all evil, let us quench it in the waters of our love ; for it is written, "charity shall cover a multitude of sins."   O ! that these simple thoughts, given you from the precious mine of truth, may bring an abundant faith in your life, and in my own, to His praise.   AMEN.

7*

THE PRODIGAL SON.

LUKE XX. 11, AND FOLLOWING VERSES.

MY DEAR FRIENDS:—I shall ask your attention at this time to the Parable of the Prodigal Son. And, first of all, I will read to you my theme.

And He said, A certain man had two sons: And the younger of them said to his father, Father, give me the portion of goods that falleth to me. And he divided unto them his living.

And not many days after, the younger son gathered all together, and took his journey into a far country, and there wasted his substance with riotous living. And when he had spent all, there arose a mighty famine in that land; and he began to be in want. And he went and joined himself to a citizen of that country; and he sent him into his fields to feed swine. And he would fain have filled his belly with the husks that the swine did eat: and no man gave unto him.

And when he came to himself, he said, How many hired servants of my father's have bread enough and to spare, and I perish with hunger! I will arise and go to

my father, and will say unto him, Father, I have sinned
against heaven, and before thee, and am no more worthy
to be called thy son: make me as one of thy hired
servants.

And he arose, and came to his father. But when he
was yet a great way off, his father saw him, and had compassion, and ran, and fell on his neck, and kissed him.
And the son said unto him, Father, I have sinned against
heaven, and in thy sight, and am no more worthy to be
called thy son.

But the father said to his servants, Bring forth the best
robe, and put it on him; and put a ring on his hand,
and shoes on his feet: and bring hither the fatted calf,
and kill it; and let us eat, and be merry: for this my
son was dead, and is alive again; he was lost, and is
found. And they began to be merry.

Now his elder son was in the field: and as he came
and drew nigh to the house, he heard music and dancing. And he called one of the servants, and asked what
these things meant. And he said unto him, Thy brother
is come; and thy father hath killed the fatted calf,
because he hath received him safe and sound. And he
was angry, and would not go in: therefore came his
father out, and entreated him. And he answering said
to his father, Lo, these many years do I serve thee, neither
transgressed I at any time thy commandment; and yet
thou never gavest me a kid, that I might make merry
with my friends: but as soon as this thy son was come,
which hath devoured thy living with harlots, thou hast
killed for him the fatted calf. And he said unto him,
Son, thou art ever with me, and all that I have is thine.
It was meet that we should make merry, and be glad:
for this thy brother was dead, and is alive again; and was
lost, and is found.

Now, let me first of all remind you, that this passage is generally applied to those who are unbelievers. I shall not so use it now. I have no doubt, that a very serviceable application may be made, from that point of view, but that is not the primal form. You cannot fail to see the force of the explanation : "A certain man had two sons." I have no doubt their experience represents, to a large extent, the experience of many thousands of God's people, after they are regenerated. I know that after I have said all that I have to say, the overtopping height of the chapter is, The unfailing grace of the Father. If Jesus had not said these boys were sons, I never should have thought it, they are so unlike their father. "The younger of them said to his father, Father, give me the portion of goods that falleth to me. And he divided unto them his living." How wonderfully gracious is God in His providential mercies to His people. How freely He opens His hand to every living creature.

You have often heard of the fall of this younger son, but I wish you to realize that his fall was in his father's house. Any man who wants God's goods instead of His presence, is a fallen man, whether he knows it or not. "Give me the portion of goods that falleth to me." What a condition this must betoken in that son's heart. I charge you to beware of the creation of a separate interest. God did not redeem you to go away from Him, but that you might live ever before Him ; and yet how true it is, you find many men, though God's children,

that can conduct their commercial affairs as though
God had no part in them. Men forget their hon-
esty, spending large sums of money without a
thought that they are stewards. From this time,
I beg you to have no separate interest from Him
who holds all things in His hand,—from the living
God. If you do not eat and drink to God's glory;
if you separate yourself from Him in anything,
you are violating the sweet relationship common
to all. Now, no sooner does this younger son
find himself possessed of the goods, than he finds
he has alienated his mind — he has emptied his
mind of the father, to make way for the wretched
goods.

"And not many days after, the younger son gathered all together, and took his journey into a *far*
country." I thank God for that word; there is no
such thing as a little departure from God,—no such
thing as a little sin. As he goes away from his
father's house, you cannot find a trace of his father's
presence. When the boy comes back, the canvas
is literally filled with his father, but there is not an
inch of ground occupied by the father as the boy
goes away. Mark you, all departure from God is
purely voluntary. God never shakes hands with
one of His children to bid them good bye; He
never stands on the departing side; He is on the
arriving side, ready to welcome the wanderer. Oh,
that I could leave with you this determination,
never to speak of God. as though He were absent.
Listen to the strong words of the fourteenth chapter of John: "If a man love Me, he will keep My

words : and My Father will love him, and we will come unto him, and make our abode with him." If the regenerated heart is not the home of God,— if He does not say, 'I will never forsake thee,' our Christianity is little better than a myth. Thank God, we have heard Him say, " Blessed is the man whom Thou choosest, * * * that he may dwell in Thy presence." I never expect to spend another moment with the idea of the absence of God in this heart, till I see Him face to face. An absent God! going away after goods! May God purge our hearts of this damnable delusion held by the children of God.—And now, he is gone.

I am not going to say much about the expression, "In riotous living;" you have heard a good deal about that. It is a dark verse, but not so dark as where he asks his father for the goods, — not so dark, because it is at the other end of night, the darkness that precedes the dawn. " And when he had spent all, there arose a mighty famine in that land ; and he began to be in want." Oh, how glad I am, how thankful ! I would that I could bring you to the sense of famine. Perhaps some of you say, 'You have not touched my experience ; I have not wasted my goods.' Perhaps not ; but you have a cold heart, you are living at a distance from your Father. So have numbers of you who profess and call yourselves Christians, and you go after the theatre and dancing and novels, in order to make up for what you think the poverty of Christianity. What, not satisfied with Jesus ! not finding in Him fullness of blessing ! Oh, I pray you be careful.

"Take heed lest there be in you an evil heart of
unbelief in departing from the living God."

Let me remind you, that when that famine came,
it was a severe one. Think of it; a child of God
living down among the swine! Ask yourselves to-
day, which is your country. "I seek a better,"
said Abraham, "even a heavenly." Cain builded a
city here, but do you think Abraham built a city
here? No, he never bought an inch of ground
except to bury his wife in; he was a stranger and
a pilgrim on earth. Let me beseech you to realize
this,—your citizenship is in heaven : and come down
out of your chamber, morning by morning, with
the spirit of the better life and the glory of the
future written on your brow. That is what is
wanted, the power of the life of Christ as a fountain
of living water.

And now, poor fellow, I think I can see him waking
up, as I wish to God others would wake up. Listen ;
"In my father's house is bread enough and to
spare." Yes, that is right, you have no thought of
the famine reaching your father's house. His judgment is all right at that point, and although he is
deeply fallen, yet truth holds him still ; and he
says, "I will arise and go to my father, and will
say unto him, Father, I have sinned against heaven,
and before thee, and am no more worthy to be
called thy son : make me as one of thy hired servants." Every man who holds a separate interest
from God, is sinning against heaven, — and mark
the form, "sinning against heaven and before thee ;
I am no more worthy to be called thy son : make

me as one of thy hired servants. And he arose,
and came to his father." Notice the resolve made,
and the resolve carried into execution. As Young
says, in his Night Thoughts, a man at thirty sus-
pects he is a fool; at forty he knows it; at fifty
resolves and re-resolves, and dies the same. Oh,
prodigal children, come home! You sat at the table
of your Lord, perhaps, but yesterday; come back
not only to the table, but to the heart of your Christ.

And now observe, "And he arose, and came to
his father. But when he was yet a great way off"
—he went into a far off land, but, blessed be God,—
"when he was yet a great way off, his father saw
him, and had compassion, and ran, and fell on his
neck, and kissed him." I have sometimes thought,
that had I been a prodigal son, well nigh breaking
my father's heart, perhaps the most difficult part
of the return would be to come up the garden walk
to the front door, — it might be on some winter's
night,—and being almost afraid to put my hand on
the knocker. I have always felt that part of the
return would be most difficult; perhaps to see my
father's shadow reflected on the blind. And how
these thoughts would come: How will he receive
me? What will he say to me? But mark, the
Lord saves His returned children all that part,—
"for when he was yet a great way off, his father
saw him." I do not believe that the eyes of the
father had been off his boy in one sense, since his
departure. Oh, I pray you, come home, prodigal
children, for your Father waits to receive you, nay,
He runs.

What a wonderful thought it is! To-day, I
doubt not that in the serene quiet of His throne,
He sits unmoved by all yonder planets and stars
whirling in their orbits. The sun, the world, the
great material universe goes on, and not a single
feature of the divine face is ruffled; but let some
wanderer desire to return, and the blessed God will
leave His throne, and run out and fall on his neck.
Wonderful teaching this! I pray that it may come
with the power of the Spirit of God to your hearts.

And now notice, the son says, "Father, I have
sinned against heaven, and in thy sight, and am no
more worthy to be called thy son." He had come
to himself; before this he had been beside himself.
When the world sees a man becoming anxious
about spiritual things, the world says, he is going
mad; but when Christ sees a man coming to Him,
He says, his madness is over. If the world is
right, then God is wrong; but if God be right, the
world is wrong indeed. And his father said, "Bring
forth the best robe, and put it on him; and put a
ring on his hand, and shoes on his feet." What!
then he had not given him all before? No; the
father has in reserve the best things. "And bring
hither the fatted calf:" note this word—the *fatted*
calf; not one that is being fatted. God was ready
and prepared.

In Nottinghill, where I reside, I have a wealthy
friend, who has, hanging in his dining-room, a
picture of the prodigal son. In the centre of the
canvas stands the father, with his long and vener-
able beard, and his rich crimson robe, testifying to

the dignity of his position ; and there lying upon his breast, is the poor tattered boy ; his bare legs tell of the weary way, and as he rests upon his father's bosom, his eyes are upturned, and you can see the tears standing in them ; and there stands a woman on one side, with arms filled with robes, and another with the shoes ; and in the background is a man bringing in the fatted calf ; and listen, "Let us eat, and be merry: for this my son was dead, and is alive again ; he was lost, and is found." Oh Christ, save this people from having any single interest away from Thee ! Let us not be dead to Thee, for we are to live with Thee for ever. Eternity is begun. Our Father in heaven hath left us to shine as lights in the darkness. Oh God, let not one of Thy children be dead towards Thee ! And now, they begin to make merry. How beautiful that is ; there is no talk about leaving off, you see. I am glad for that word ; I am thankful for it. God understands merriment. To many men, God is a cast-iron being, with a rod in His hand. How I would like to smash that idea into atoms. And now notice, you will see no reference to the atonement of Christ in this chapter, for it is taken for granted that the relationship of these children will bring it to mind.

"Now his elder son was in the field : and as he came and drew nigh to the house, he heard music and dancing." Methinks if I were to go to my father's house, and heard music and dancing, I should not care to call a servant and ask its meaning. "Thy brother is come; and thy father hath killed the fatted calf, because he hath received him safe and sound." What, not a word about the loss of character or property? Is that what God says? Why, sirs, what is property to *the boy*? What does God think of money in comparison with the soul? God grant that all may learn the truth of the importance of the souls of men. I would rather have spoken the last few weeks to the people of your cities, than have transacted the commerce of the world for the last fifty years. Sunday School teachers, remember the glory of your work; let not your service be lukewarm, and God will bless you in your labor.

Some of my hearers may say to themselves, 'You have not sketched my character in the younger son.' Well, perhaps I shall find you in the elder. This son was living with his father, and no doubt he was exceedingly scrupulous about the hedges, for he did not want the neighbors' cattle in his father's garden. After coming in from the field, he hears music, and asks the reason of it. "Oh, thy brother is come!" "What is that to me?" We have hundreds of so-called Christians in the church, who, while they will give thousands of dollars to build a material structure, have not a tithe of interest in the saving of souls. I have known parents—I have in my mind this moment such parents—as cold-hearted as that. A dear girl said to me, "Can you tell me if I am a Christian?" "Why do you ask?" I said. "I have been a member of this church for six years," and she burst into tears. "You understand me, sir, I don't want to

speak a word against my dear papa and mamma ;
but at home we never say one word about this
thing from month's end to month's end."

There is nothing to compare with the coldness
of the elder son. Oh, sirs, a "sneak thief" is an
honest man to such a spirit as that. And notice,
"He was angry, and would not go in: therefore
came his father out, and entreated him." That
word *out*, bespeaks it. The father—blessed be God
—the father came out and entreated him ; and "he
answering said to his father, Lo, these many years
do I serve thee." What! do I read this aright?
Oh, I see, I understand: I thought you were a son,
but you *serve;* aye, you are a *servant!* I serve
thee many years. You miserable fellow,—"*serve*
thee," — the old carping spirit of the old Pharisees
brought to life. "I *serve* thee, neither transgressed
I at any time thy commandment," that other boy
did, but I never, "and yet thou never gavest me a
kid." Do you see the comparison between the kid
and the calf ? Why, you wretch, if you had a kid,
1 don't think you have got two friends that you
could invite to dinner. Out upon you, son, as I
think of these things, for they are most melancholy
and terribly true. But listen ; the father says,
"Son, thou art ever with me," — you see he is not
moved one particle,—"and all that I have is thine.
It was meet that we should make merry, and be
glad." *It was meet*, do you hear this, elder son?
Oh, you miserable, carping fellow ! "Devoured thy
living with harlots !" How do you know that ? I ask
each serving one of you, if you have never done it

before, just come and say, Lord, I am ashamed of myself, for ever having any separate interests from Thee. I will never dare to believe for one moment of my future life, that Thou art absent from me. On the cold stones of the London market, buying sheep and bullocks, I recall those times when I have had the most blessed communion with God. Blessed unity, from this time never separate again. The Lord strengthen you! God the Spirit reveal to you the Father, and from this time may you never acknowledge a separate interest from Him who says, "I ascend to My Father and your Father, and to My God and your God!" AMEN.

8

THE TWENTY-THIRD PSALM.

NO doubt you are all familiar with this Psalm. The word of God is an inexhaustible mine of truth. When we read any other book often, no matter how good, it tires, but not so the Word of the living God. It is intended to show us, that God's Word was not intended to be considered with the intelligence alone ; it is a living power, and it needs to be read, marked, learned, and inwardly digested, and a continual desire for God's Word is the chief characteristic of the true child of God. Christ, in the integrity of His character, is embodied in this book, and in proportion as we make its truths our own, in the same proportion does it change us from glory to glory.

"The Lord is my shepherd, I shall not want." Why does David, the sweet singer of Israel, say he shall not want? Is it because he is chief magistrate of the people? Millions of money were gathered by the Psalmist, in order to erect Solomon's temple, and yet so intrenched by position and wealth, he does not say that he shall not want because of his position, but because of the faithfulness of the Lord. The argument that applied to the Psalmist, applies with equal force to us. The reason we may say we shall not want, is because the Lord is our shepherd; because His faithfulness fails not. It is this;—Jesus said, 'Your heavenly Father knoweth ye have need of these things; and which of you by taking thought can add one cubit to your stature? If ye are not able then to do the things which are least, why take thought for the rest?' Christ said, 'Consider the lilies of the field, they toil not, neither do they spin ; yet I say unto you, that even Solomon in all his glory was not arrayed like one of these.' Oh, let us, more joyfully looking into the future, say, I shall not want, because the Lord is my shepherd. He gives, not because of our poverty, but of His wealth. Don't let unbelief project troubles into the future! Unbelief can foresee coming difficulties that never come at all. I venture to say, you have all had such experiences as these.

A word about the shepherd. The Lord Jesus Christ says, " I am the good shepherd ; the good shepherd giveth His life for the sheep." We are "the sheep of His pasture," then, because He has bought us with His precious blood; not for anything we have done or can do. Nothing of that kind on our part can establish any relationship between us and Him.

We are not only His by purchase, but because God has made us ; and we are kept by Him as the delegated depository of Christ, who prayed, " Holy

Father, keep through Thine own name those whom I have committed to Thee." It is one of the profound stays of my being, that in my utter weakness, I am yet Christ's deposit in the hands of the eternal Father, and He has asked Him to keep me. "The Lord is my shepherd." It is part of a shepherd's business to keep.

"He maketh me to lie down in green pastures: He leadeth me beside the still waters." Notice the present tense in this Psalm:—that word "maketh." It is as though the hand of God had been put on the head of His child in his unrest and disquiet. He knows that the journey is too great; knows our dependence on Him, and *maketh* us lie down and rest. And turning back in your experience, you should not be surprised at this. "He maketh me." Why? Because He knows how wearing our sorrow becomes; because His joy is too great for us. Look at the lowliness of the position, — the dependence, — but it is in green pastures, not in a wilderness: there the fragrant herbage is springing on every side; and by "the still waters," where the water of life, like a broad river, is meandering its way beside the pathway of human history. Blessed is the man who trusts his Lord, for he shall be like a tree planted near the water, stretching out its roots to the river. "Ye shall not care for the year of drought," think of that! Not safe for a week, or a month, or a year, but forever! When the earth is dry and the rain does not come, there is the secret supply from the river, and where all else fails, there is no failure here, if it is by the still waters.

"He restoreth my soul." How beautiful that
word is. He does it now. Is there one here who
has the consciousness that he is far from being
restored. Perhaps he has been trodden down,
trying to bloom in some desolate place. Do I
speak to a dear child in the midst of an unconverted family? Do I speak to a wife who finds
her path difficult? Do I speak to a backslider?
Let me tenderly talk to you. In a meeting I
attended near London, among the crowd I noticed
a man standing near a pillar. I saw the interest
on his face, and was pained to see him leave with
the rest when the meeting was ended. That night,
as I was going to London, I met this man at the
station; how delighted I was. I said, "Are you a
child of God?" He answered, "I was once."
"What do you mean," said I, "God is not apt to
turn His children adrift." He replied; "Twelve
years ago I had a fall, through drink." "What," I
asked, "and in twelve years have you never been
restored?" "Yes," he answered, "but my life has
been in doubt." I found he was going in the same
direction that I was, and I invited him into the
carriage with me.

Taking out this book, I opened it to the passage
I am dwelling on now, "He *restoreth* my soul," and
said to him:— "I bring God's word of faith to you,
adapted to your experience, not as an inquirer,
but as a backslider. That is His remedy for your
present condition. I pray you, believe He restoreth your soul, *because He says so,* and I am as sure
as we are riding to-night together, that you will be

restored." He hesitated, thinking it too good to be true. I said, "Suppose you have a daughter about eighteen years old, who has given you a good deal of trouble the last year; suppose she has confessed her wickedness to her mother, and you are aware of it; what would you say? Would you say, Dear wife, let us restore her in six months?" "No," said the man. "In three months?" said I. "No." "In one month?" "No, immediately." "Oh!" I replied, "you are better than the Lord, are you? Come, my brother, you must get rid of that thought:" and in the carriage we knelt together, and he was restored. He restoreth my soul; why, dear friends, I believe my Father has restored my soul twenty times to-day. I believe He is doing it now. If it were not for His restoration, I believe I should be a chronic backslider. We want a power to lean on. What would He do with His strength, if we were not to lean on Him? "He restoreth my soul;" this is not mere sentiment. As a commercial man of a good deal of experience, I am free to say, of all places where I have enjoyed communion with God, that intercourse in the halls of commerce has been most precious. After a day's work, you are sure to be depressed; look up for the restoring grace. As a gardener, with his watering-pot in the evening, restores the drooping plants, even thus you shall know the restoration of divine grace.

Then "He leadeth me in the paths of righteousness for His name's sake." Listen while I tell them over in order; He maketh, He leadeth, He restoreth. "Leadeth me in the paths of righteousness for His name's sake." Do some of you say, the distress of my life is because there is so little practical righteousness coming out of my life? When I have been walking with God, I have never needed to look for open doors, or to open them. When you are prepared for work, God gives it. I could sooner believe the sun would not rise, than that when we are ready, God will not use us. There are some Christians, who in walking with God, in communion with Him, maintain the keen edge of their life ; but the Christian with blunted edge is dulled, and God's nature would sooner change, than such a man be used. The boundary of our usefulness is marked off at the point of our surrender to God. If you are not used more, it is because you are not fitted. I am not touching the question of natural gifts and capacity. I am touching the question of personal fitness for the Master's service.

"Yea, though I walk through the valley of the shadow of death, I will fear no evil." Some have seen a great deal of darkness in that verse. "Yea, though I walk through the valley of the shadow." I never heard a more lovely expression; it is the valley of *shadow*, that is all. Up to this point the Psalmist has been speaking about God, now he is talking with Him. You cannot speak about God, but He must come. He says, "Where two or three are gathered together in My name, there am I." Again, "For thou art with me, Thy rod and Thy staff they comfort me." A word about the rod and staff. I know some think it necessary that God should deal out much of discipline, but it is not the obedient children that are punished, I am persuaded, if you take His yoke. "Take My yoke upon you;" you cannot wear two yokes; reject your own, and you will find 'His yoke is easy, and His burden is light.' His rod, not merely to discipline,—surely the idea of stay and comfort is here.

How wonderful the later strokes of this Psalm are. How would the courage be taken out of our enemies, were a banqueting table constantly spread before them. They would say, "Those men cannot be very fearful." God spreads such a table in the presence of our mortal enemies, death, sin, temptation. He stands and says, "Take, eat; this is My body, which is broken for you; this is My blood, shed for many." "Thou preparest a table before me in the presence of mine enemies: Thou anointest mine head with oil." Simon, the Pharisee, might neglect this part of Eastern hospitality, but a guest of the Lord will not fail to have His head anointed with oil. His joy shall stream from thine head to thy feet, as thou sittest in His banqueting-house, and His banner over thee is love.

I have sometimes felt almost unequal to talking of this last clause, "My cup runneth over." Do not think me irreverent, if I say that Jesus goes from guest to guest, looks into each cup, and finding it partially empty, does not trust to servants, but Himself filleth it, so that it runneth over; nor does He mind spoiling the table-cloth with its overflow of profuseness, so boundless is His love. "My

cup runneth over. Surely goodness and mercy
shall follow me." How often we hear that word
from the lips of men, "surely." What are we sure
of? We have a proverb in England, "Nothing
is sure but death." But we have this promise,
"Surely goodness and mercy," these two attendant
ministers of God, who stand on either side of our
history, day by day; "surely goodness and mercy
shall follow me." Your business is to hedge in the
days as they pass. "Shall follow me," mark this,
"*all* the days," not some, not the days when the
sun shines; not the marriage morning; but in all
days, by the couch of the suffering, and by the
fresh dug grave; "follow me all the days of my
life." Oh, suffering, afflicted children of God,
pierce this cloud, for remember how Bunyan in his
prison sings:

> ' For though they shut this outward man,
>   Within their bolts and bars ;
> By faith in Christ, I yet can mount,
>   Far higher than the stars.'

Oh, blessed be God for the power He has given
us to say, "All the days of my life." "And I will
dwell * * for ever," not in my earthly possessions,
not on David's throne for ever, but "in the house
of the Lord," that house, "beautiful for situation,
the joy of the whole earth;" the house which
Christ promised, when He said, "I go to prepare a
place for you." Do you ever meditate on that
thought? Think, for eighteen hundred years, the
power and wisdom and might of our Lord has been
used in providing a house for His people. "I go to

prepare a place for you. And * * I will come again, and receive you unto myself ; that where I am, there ye may be also;" and we are waiting till He comes. Oh, blessed God! we thank Thee for Thy Spirit, who bridges the way for us ; we thank Thee for the angels, who conduct us across, and while we long for " the robes of whiteness;" and "the starry crown," we sing :

> " Oh eyes that are weary, and hearts that are sore,
> Look off unto Jesus, and sorrow no more."

Have you learned this ? God help you to learn it ! Why put it off till the vision breaks on your astonished gaze. God help you to believe, for it is written : "If ye will not believe, surely ye shall not be established." And may God make this seed Psalm grow into a harvest, not of thirty, sixty, or one hundred, but of ten thousand-fold in the future history of your life.

THE SECRET OF POWER.

MARK, Chapter IX.

NOTHING is more interesting to the true follower of the Lord Jesus Christ, than to note
how He dealt with His disciples, when He
was with them on earth. Human nature is the
same in all ages ; I doubt not that much might be
done by education and civilization, but you will
always find the tendency to evil, that is common in
one age, common in another, and common to their
descendants. I trust many of us who are here,
desire that God should use us very much. I think
that we cannot have a more helpful thought than
this, — what Jesus Christ can do with this being of
mine, when it is surrendered wholly to Him. It is
astonishing what an able workman can do with a
bad tool ; it is not so much the tool as the workman
we look at. It is a blessed thing to be made the
tool of the Lord. And shall a man boast ? Shall
the axe boast of itself ? Did I not cut that tree
down splendidly ?

What great thoughts there are in the Bible! It is full of wisdom and interest, and one of the chapters among many deeply interesting, is the ninth chapter of Mark. Let us consider a portion of it. "And * * Jesus taketh with Him Peter, and James, and John, and leadeth them up into a high mountain apart by themselves; and He was transfigured before them." Consecrated men, in a position of eminence, did you ever notice how constantly Christ takes with Him Peter, and James, and John? And it is to teach us that consecrated men see Christ's work and example. Take the case of the daughter of Jairus. When the Master arrived at the house, the hired mourners were wailing, and Christ said, "Why make ye this ado, and weep?" Christ never rebukes sorrow, but He does not like people to cry at so much an hour. And so He said, "The damsel is not dead, but sleepeth;" and they laughed, though they were crying two minutes before; but it makes no difference to them, they can laugh or cry, whichever they are paid for.

"And His raiment became shining, exceeding white as snow; so as no fuller on earth can white them. And there appeared unto them Elias with Moses: and they were talking with Jesus." He knew them; He had been with Moses at the bush; He had been with Elijah on the Mount; they were old companions. "Peter answered and said to Jesus, Master, it is good for us to be here: and let us make three tabernacles; one for Thee, and one for Moses, and one for Elias. For he wist not what to say; for they were sore afraid. And there

was a cloud that overshadowed them : and a voice
came out of the cloud, saying, This is My beloved
Son: hear Him." What a group of dignitaries
assembled there ! I do not wonder they scarcely
knew what they were doing. Father, Son, the
manifesting glory of Jesus, and Moses, and Elias.

Notice what follows: " And suddenly, when they
had looked round about, they saw no man any
more, save Jesus only with themselves. And as
they came down from the mountain, He charged
them that they should tell no man what things
they had seen, till the Son of man were risen from
the dead. And they kept that saying with themselves, questioning one with another what the rising
from the dead should mean. And they asked Him,
saying, Why say the scribes that Elias must first
come? And he answered and told them, Elias
verily cometh first, and restoreth all things ; and
how it is written of the Son of man, that He must
suffer many things, and be set at naught. But I
say unto you, that Elias is indeed come, and they
have done unto him whatsoever they listed, as it is
written of him. And when He came to His disciples, He saw a great multitude about them, and the
scribes questioning with them." And the memory
of that blessed voice that woke them up, how
beautiful it is in the direction of self-abeyance, to
have Him say, " This is My beloved Son: hear
Him." If you would know the heart of Jesus, you
must be alone with Him.

" And as they came down from the mountain,
He charged them that they should tell no man

what things they had seen, till the Son of man were risen from the dead." They did not know what it meant, and it was not peculiar to them; the ignorance of many is as dense in our day. I don't suppose fifty in this house are living in the power of the resurrection of the dead. I pray God continually to give me power to know it. " That ye may know," said Paul, " what is the exceeding greatness of His power to us-ward who believe, according to the working of His mighty power, which He wrought in Christ, when He raised Him from the dead."

And now notice the change in the fourteenth verse: " And when He came to His disciples, He saw a great multitude about them, and the scribes questioning with them. And straightway all the people, when they beheld Him, were greatly amazed, and running to Him saluted Him. And He asked the scribes, What question ye with them? And one of the multitude answered and said, Master, I have brought unto Thee my son, which hath a dumb spirit; and wheresoever he taketh him, he teareth him; and he foameth, and gnasheth with his teeth, and pineth away: and I spake to Thy disciples that they should cast him out; and they could not." Oh, blessed Master! we do praise Thee, that the glory of the summit had not sufficient attractions to keep Thee up there; we are glad that the devil-possessed boy, and the sinners at the foot of the mountain, had stronger claims than glory upon Thee. May we see the alternation, and realize by faith that we are coming to Mount Zion, and that

Thou didst come down for a season of blessed
confidence to a sin-stained world. May we learn
that the life in heaven is the death of the life here.
God grant we may know what it is to follow Christ
in this thing.

The disciples were unable to cast out this evil
spirit. Why was this ? They had received power
to do it. It is written, in the sixth chapter, "And
He called unto Him the twelve, and began to
send them forth by two and two ; and gave them
power over unclean spirits." In another place
we are told, "And they cast out many devils,
and anointed with oil many that were sick, and
healed them." And in a third passage we learn,
that the seventy "returned again with joy, saying,
Lord, even the devils are subject unto us through
Thy name." They came back to tell Christ, glory-
ing in these results. We observe, He sent them
out two and two, and they cast out devils, healed
the sick, and preached the gospel. At the point
where we are, they are not two and two, but were
all gathered together ; they had power when they
were two and two, but now that they are gathered
together, they have not power to cast out this one
evil spirit. How do you account for that ? Here,
in the sixth chapter, we are told they are strong,
and possessed of great power, and now, when they
are all together, they had not the power to cast
out one evil spirit ! How is this ? We shall find
out.

"He answereth him, and saith, O faithless generation, how long shall I be with you ? how long

shall I suffer you? bring him unto Me. And
they brought him unto Him: and when he saw
Him, straightway the spirit tare him; and he fell
on the ground, and wallowed foaming. And He
asked his father, How long is it ago since this came
unto him? And he said, Of a child. And ofttimes
it hath cast him into the fire, and into the waters,
to destroy him: but if Thou canst do any thing,
have compassion on us, and help us. Jesus said
unto him, If thou canst believe, all things are
possible to him that believeth. And straightway
the father of the child cried out, and said with
tears, Lord, I believe; help Thou mine unbelief."

How different is this prayer of the father's from
the unwise prayer of the disciples. In one place
they said, "Lord, increase our faith." And was
not that wise? you ask. It was not wise for them
to say it, for He said, 'If ye have faith, and doubt
not, * * ye shall say unto this mountain, Be thou
removed, and be thou cast into the sea; it shall be
done.' It is better to be honest and say, Lord, the
season of unbelief has come. Some Christians
think that God keeps a sort of apothecary's shop,
with faith and grace and goodness done up in
bottles, and if we ask Him for them, He will
deliver them. I don't believe this; faith is a grace
that grows, and when you don't use what you have,
you cannot expect it to grow. The father put it
rightly, when he said, "Lord, I believe; help Thou
mine unbelief."

"When Jesus saw that the people came running
together, He rebuked the foul spirit, saying unto

him, Thou dumb and deaf spirit, I charge thee,
come out of him, and enter no more into him.
And the spirit cried, and rent him sore, and came
out of him: and he was as one dead; insomuch
that many said, He is dead. But Jesus took him
by the hand, and lifted him up; and he arose." I
wish to have you see, that what the disciples
cannot accomplish together, the Master accom-
plishes alone with ease. Dear friends, this is a
great lesson. Do you remember the seven sons of
Sceva, who pretended to cast out evil spirits, and
the evil spirit set upon them, and they were glad
to get away? The evil spirit says, "Jesus I know,
and Paul I know; but who are ye?" If you are
not a Christian character, the devil won't care for
you in the least. I speak not in any idle boast,
but the sooner the devil knows I am set for Jesus,
as one of his adversaries, the better I shall be
pleased. The battle for God is no child's play!
"We wrestle not against flesh and blood, but
against principalities, against powers, against the
rulers of the darkness of this world."

It was not always so with these disciples, as I
have shown you in the sixth chapter. But a lapse
of faith had come; all men come to that point in
their spiritual life. If you do not fight the good
fight of faith, if you are half God's child and half
devil's child,—if you fail to rid yourselves of those
damnable influences, you will never know the power
of the life of Christ. Put away from you those
things that are blasting the life of Christ. How
grateful I should be if the Master would come and

exorcise every dumb spirit. Hundreds of Christians can talk very volubly on any other subject, but speak of Christ, and they are dumb; they can talk about the events of the day, but as for talking of Christ, they cannot. This thing is so solemnly true, that my heart is filled with sorrow and heaviness about it.

"He is dead," they said; Oh no, you need not fear that! "Jesus took him by the hand, and lifted him up; and he arose. And when He was come into the house, His disciples asked Him privately, Why could not we cast him out?" That is right; having come to that point, we shall have a lesson. It is beautiful to see how He deals with them. He said, "This kind cometh forth by nothing, but by prayer and fasting." What is that, by abstinence from food? No, I don't think it is. I know I could not abstain from food very much. I am sure it is not that. We must not leave out the beautiful thought suggested by the word 'prayer.' As Montgomery says:

"Prayer is the Christian's vital breath!"

Always living in a prayerful spirit, you get into secret converse with Jesus naturally. One calls on another, and he gives him an hour of valuable time, but he has not ten minutes to give to Christ. Suppose a man were to lock himself up in his counting-room, and say to his clerk, If any one wants to see me, I am engaged for ten minutes in communion with the Lord Jesus Christ. They would think he had taken leave of his senses, and

would have him in a lunatic asylum directly. And
yet he wastes time on some wretched political
affair. If you could see them standing in one
dense mass in the London Exchange, you would
think all the interests of England and America
were at stake, and if they could only get Gladstone
to do that, or D'Israeli to do the other, the Millennium would come directly; and they get it; and
the Millennium —— does not come!

And now notice the thirty-third verse: "And
He came to Capernaum: and being in the house
He asked them, What was it that ye disputed
among yourselves by the way?" Oh Master, how
we do rejoice that Thou knowest how to touch the
vital question. I put these two scenes together,
because they are part of the whole. When they
were come to Capernaum, they came into a house,
doubtless for refreshment, and when the Master
was with them there, He asked them, "What
was it that ye disputed among yourselves by the
way? But they held their peace: for by the way
they had disputed among themselves, who should
be the greatest." Oh, I see, I see, that is what it
was; you could not cast the devil out, because he
was in. The devil does not cast himself out when
he enthrones himself in the heart; there he is, and
the devil does not cast out Satan. That is the
mischief, you see, and the Master knows the working of it all, and touches the whole thing at once.
What were ye disputing by the way? They were
disputing about who should be greatest. "And
He sat down, and called the twelve, and saith unto

them, If any man desire to be first, the same shall
be last of all, and servant of all." If you would be
the greatest, take the lowest place of all. The
world sticks a man on a pedestal, and says, "Now,
you common men, come and worship." The Lord
says, "If any man desire to be first, the same shall
be last of all, and servant of all." In proportion as
you are used of God, you will come down, down,
down. Many a man gifted of God, instead of leaning on the Master, thinks he is something, and he
is nothing. A friend said to me, "I got into a
great trouble last week." "How is that?" "I got
puffed up with pride, and the devil got hold of me."
"I am not surprised," I said. "I got no relief," he
continued, "till I found this passage, 'If a man
think himself to be something, when he is nothing,
he deceiveth himself,' and the moment I read that,
I got free, for the devil cannot hold nothing." A
great truth quaintly put.

Jesus "took a child, and set him in the midst of
them: and when He had taken him in His arms,
He said unto them, Whosoever shall receive one of
such children in My name, receiveth Me; and
whosoever shall receive Me, receiveth not Me, but
Him that sent Me." Dear friends, this unsightly
thing of desire for prominence in the disciples, is
not confined to any one place. On one occasion,
Christ had to say, "The kings of the Gentiles exercise lordship over them; * * but ye shall not be
so: but he that is greatest among you, let him be
as the younger; and he that is chief, as he that
doth serve." We don't rule in the church of God

by the assumption of prerogative, but we do rule by serving. Aspire to be a Pope, or an elder, or a deacon, and you will discover before long that the discomforts and troubles attendant on your ambitious designs are far greater than you have any idea of. But I will tell you what I have lived long enough to find out; that if you love a person very much, and try to serve them, they will let you do anything you like; you "stoop to conquer." May we be just as little children, that we may be greatest of all; a little child is simple and guileless."

Let me remind you of the following: "And John answered Him, saying, Master, we saw one casting out devils in Thy name, and he followeth not us." What do you mean? Do you mean in the contention, my brother? Followed not us! a nice following indeed! *My* church! *My* people! How I would like to see the church of God purged of that! When we get where we can rejoice at the prosperity of others, then God will greatly prosper us. When I can rejoice in the prosperity of my dear brother Hepworth, or Cameron, then I have reached a point where God can trust me somewhat. How often Christians remain contented in this unhappy state. I meet a brother and say, "How are you getting on?" "Oh, very well." "Have you had any additions to your church lately?" "Well, no, not many in the past three months, or, come to think of it, in six months." "Well, how are your prayer-meetings?" "Oh, that is the difficulty; we cannot get our people out to prayer-meetings." " What do you mean by getting along pretty well?

If you were a business man, and were asked how you were doing, would you say, Oh, pretty well, but we have not had any trade for the last six months ? You would not talk like that." And that is what is the trouble with many churches. If you should ask a jury of business men to give a verdict on the condition of such churches, they would say they were in a condition of spiritual bankruptcy.

I have sometimes said to a brother, How is so-and-so doing in your town, (perhaps an evangelical clergyman, who, I knew, had been doing a good work,) and he says, "I don't know anything about him," and in a few minutes you will find a considerable jealousy. I would to God, that those who profess and call themselves Christians, would see that another twelve-hours does not elapse before they purge themselves from this sin. Listen: "Let nothing be done through strife or vainglory ; but in lowliness of mind let each esteem other better than themselves." Jesus said, in reply to His disciples' question, "Forbid him not : for there is no man which shall do a miracle in My name, that can lightly speak evil of Me."

Blessed Lord, let us take heed to the Master's solemn words ! Grant that we may learn to follow His paths, and ever walk in the steps of His most holy life !

THOUGHTS.

I HATE . . . . THOUGHTS : BUT THY LAW DO I LOVE.

YOU will find the basis or starting-point of my address in the one hundred and nineteenth Psalm and one hundred and thirteenth verse. I am going to talk about thoughts. You will observe this word, "I hate thoughts." Did you ever read this verse before? Perhaps you will say there is not such a verse in the Bible, and I shall not be surprised if you say I have left out a word, "I hate vain thoughts." No, I have not left out a word. The word *vain* is supplied by the translators. I wish they had left it in its native ruggedness, — "I hate thoughts : but Thy law do I love." The word 'law' is not to be understood in any contracted sense, but for the whole mind of God ; and rightly understood, means, I hate the natural uprisings of thoughts that come to my mind, but God's thought, God's mind, God's breathings of the heart, I love.

Let me at once say, I thoroughly endorse the
Psalmist's statement here ; for I freely confess, that
if I could, I never would think another thought of
mine so long as I live,—I say, *if I could,* because I
am conscious of my infirmity in this respect.
There is not a soul here, but must come, sooner or
later, to that rugged statement, 'I hate thoughts.'
The influence of this may be illustrated in one or
two sentences. Suppose a telegraph boy should
come into this room at this moment, and bring
news to one of you, that some dear friend is
dangerously ill. It is but a sentence, but in that
thought is enough to destroy all of rest, and possibly all of profit to you in this meeting. Let a
business man, as he sits here, know that a firm in
which he is a creditor to the amount of fifteen or
twenty thousand dollars has just failed, and that
man's peace of mind is gone. If, for example,
some husband, living perhaps in the suburbs of the
city, allows some word of unkindness to escape his
lips, if his wife is a true woman, I'll venture to say
she has little of quiet or rest till she has seen her
husband, or put it right. So dependent are we on
thought. It is not the amount of money that
makes you rich, but the amount of thought you
possess. If I were asked for a description of
divine life, I should say, divine life is the aggregate
of divine thoughts. God says, 'Man shall not live
by bread alone, but by every word that proceedeth
out of the mouth of God.' Do you remember how
the devil came to Christ after the forty days' fast,
and asked Him why He did not turn the stones

into bread. What was His reply? " It is written, Man shall not live by bread alone, but by every word that proceedeth out of the mouth of God."

The reason of this startling statement is not far to seek. Look at the sixth chapter of Genesis: " And God saw that the wickedness of man was great in the earth, and that every imagination of the thoughts of his heart was only evil continually." Since man's fall, the human heart has only been capable of the outcome of wickedness,—remember that. This is solemnly testified by the living God. And the Hebrew word is even stronger ; it means not only the natural imagination, but man's heart is evil and evil continually. Notice another thing, that this solemn testimony from the sixth chapter of Genesis, is corroborated by Jesus Christ. Turn to the fifteenth chapter of Matthew and nineteenth verse, and hear what the Master Himself says : " For out of the heart proceed evil thoughts, murders, adulteries, fornications, thefts, false witness, blasphemies." Mark the words that stand at the head of the list. What ? Evil thoughts ! I defy any one in this house to commit sin, till the desires of his corrupt heart suggest it to him. No man has ever stolen without corrupt thought ; and so of every form of sin, it is altogether of corrupt desire : and therefore preachers speak of God's children as having escaped the corruption that is in the world through lust, that is, inordinate desire. I know men who deny the great truth of the depravity of the human mind, and will disbelieve this statement, but we have to do, not with likes or dislikes, but

9

the solemn testimony of the living God, not one jot
or tittle of which can ever fail.

And I may corroborate this position by further
testimony. Look at the word of God in the fifty-
fifth chapter of Isaiah and seventh verse. I com-
mend this verse to your thoughtful notice. " Let
the wicked forsake his way, and the unrighteous
man his thoughts : and let him return unto the
Lord, and He will have mercy upon Him ; and to
our God, for He will abundantly pardon." Here is
the promise, to one full of corrupt thoughts. Follow this again ! if any one of you are ignorant
concerning the way of salvation :—" Let the wicked
forsake his way, and the unrighteous man his
thoughts: and let him return unto the Lord, and
He will have mercy upon him ; and to our God,
for He will abundantly pardon. For My thoughts
are not your thoughts, neither are your ways My
ways, saith the Lord." If you say your thoughts
are as God's, you call Him a liar.

If there is such a wonderful contrast, if our
thoughts by nature are so corrupt and unlike the
thoughts of God, then it is wisdom to minimize the
thoughts natural to me, and fill my mind with
God's thoughts. Nature abhors a vacuum, and
just so is it of grace ; and the reason why many
Christians are not rejoicing in Christ, is because
the mind of Christ does not dwell in them.

Perhaps I am addressing some who are making
their minds cesspools of unclean thoughts. Take
heed what ye read, for the secret of the want of
joy of Christian life, is from the fact that many are

feeding on husks. I don't expect a man that is a
corpse, to walk about; and till men are quickened
by the Spirit of God, they are gravitating from
earthly to sensual, and from sensual to devilish.

And now I want you to look at another portion of
the divine Word; The second book of Kings and
fifth chapter gives the history of Naaman, who
was a leper; a little maid in his house told him if
he would go to Samaria, and see God's prophet
Elisha, he would recover him of his leprosy; and
he came in his chariot and stood before Elisha's
door, "and Elisha sent a messenger unto him, saying, Go and wash in Jordan seven times, and thy
flesh shall come again to thee, and thou shalt be
clean." Observe the words spoken by Elisha, and
representing God's mind. Observe, "But Naaman
was wroth, and went away, and said, Behold, I
thought,——" aye, here it is ; what business have
you to think? But seeing you have begun, what
did you think? — "I thought, He will surely come
out to me." I see, you are a big man. 'I did not
think Elisha would send a messenger to me; I am
next in command to the king of Syria.' I see,
Naaman, you thought Elisha was like an Egyptian
necromancer. I am glad you have spoken your
thoughts; they are better out than in.

It is a great mistake, to suppose that we can
dictate how God shall act. What would you think
of a man sending for a physician, if he were sick
with some dreadful fever, and saying, 'Doctor,
I know something of medicine, and unless you
prescribe as I want you to, I won't take your medi-

cine.' What would the physician do? He would walk out of the house. But in spiritual things, these poor, deluded, blinded sinners would dictate to God. Therefore, let every man forsake his thoughts. I hear this Syrian say, "Are not Abana and Pharpar, rivers of Damascus, better than all the waters of Israel? may I not wash in them, and be clean?" No, if you want to be clean, you must wash in Jordan. 'I thought!' let that personal pronoun 'I,' come down, for it is a wretched gathering up of men's thoughts. 'I thought!' What a contrast between his words and those we started with.

Now let us look at the one hundred and thirty-ninth Psalm and seventeenth verse: "How precious also are Thy thoughts unto me, O God!" Look at the beautiful contrast between "I hate thoughts" of mine, but listen, "How precious also are Thy thoughts unto me, O God!" Them, I love; them, I embrace; them, I value. Oh, to have the mind and heart furnished with thoughts of God. Observe what follows: "How great is the sum of them! If I should count them, they are more in number than the sand." What a beautiful expression! "When I awake, I am still with Thee." It looks as though David had begun to count the thoughts of God. When he went out in the evening to meditate, the thoughts of God crowded so fast on his mind, that he became tired and fell asleep. "If I should count them, they are more in number than the sand," and now, "when I awake, I am still with Thee."

Oh, the wealth of God's thoughts, how wonderful
they are. Remember how the holy men of old
spoke about the Word of God. John says, 'I esteem the Word of God more than food.' Jeremiah
says, 'I have found the Word, and I eat it.' And
none of these had much of the Bible. If they had
had Matthew, Mark, Luke, and the rest, I think
they would have been hardly able to contain themselves. This is the food God has given to His
children, and yet this is the loaf they so seldom
eat. As the Church of England has it, it should
be read, marked, learned, and inwardly digested.
You need not wonder your life is not what it should
be, when you think of what you feed upon. It is a
great life to live, to be sweetly filled with the Word
of the living God. Let the Word of Christ dwell
in you, sing and make melody in your hearts unto
God.

Be careful, lest you allow thoughts of distrust of
God to annoy you. Remember His promise is in
such words as these : " Be careful for nothing," but
with praise and thanksgiving, let your life be formed
by the Word of God, and the peace of God which
passeth all understanding shall be yours. One
man says, My wealth keeps me comfortable and
happy. I am sorry to hear that. Another says,
My poverty makes me wretched. I am sorry to
hear that also. The eternal God is superior to
either wealth or poverty. He that believeth that
his thoughts are as God's thoughts, calleth God a
liar. You can allow thoughts to rise in you, the
outcoming of which will impeach the integrity of

the Most High! If there is a single soul in this house, not rejoicing in the salvation of Christ, it is because you are deliberately putting God's thoughts away from you. He declares, "He that believeth on the Son hath everlasting life. This is God's thought; read it, and let it rest in your mind, and as God lives you are saved.

In your relations to your fellow-men, be careful. How often the thought of jealousy is in the heart ; God says, "Love your enemies, do good to them which hate you." Instead of being mean and selfish, receive His thoughts. He will tell you that it is in vain for you to rise up early, or tarry up late, for He gives His beloved sleep. The meaning of this is, that when you and I sleep, the great Head of the house, Christ, as a Son in His own house, is providing all our necessaries ; for "My God shall supply all your need according to His riches in glory by Christ Jesus."

One or two more words and I have done. Remember this ; that evil thoughts come continually to the unregenerated heart. I can hear you say, ' You have touched a topic that brings me much sorrow. I have found myself strangely unable to forgive my enemies.' You might well utter David's prayer, " Set a watch, O Lord, before my mouth ; keep the door of my lips ; " for "out of the abundance of the heart the mouth speaketh." That is the reason so many Christians are dumb about Christ, — they are cold ; they speak from the outcome of the heart when it is filled with divine love. Go often to the Word of God ; take heed that seeds

of righteousness are sown, that you may not depart
from God. I do not believe my heart is "prone to
wander." So far as my unregenerated heart is
concerned, that is true ; but since Christ has given
me a new heart, that heart is true to Him, and I
have a new heart and right spirit. I would not
insult my Maker, by saying His gift was prone to
wander from Him. "Take heed, brethren, lest
there be in any of you an evil heart of unbelief, in
departing from the living God." There comes the
question of evil thoughts, — where do they come
from? First, from the inherent corruption common
to all, but uncommon to those who keep the Christ-
life to the front. You are as a man, or woman, with
two lives in you, since you have become God's ;
the spirit-life is developed, and if you want it to be
developed, you must keep the foot of your spiritual
life on the neck of the flesh. The two opposites
cannot be found together. God help you in keeping
the spiritual life.

Let me remind you further, that a great many
evil thoughts are voluntarily received. When
people speak about unholy things, do not listen ;
when you see in the papers wretched items, the
result of the reading of which is to defile you, put
them into the fire. What do you mean by bringing
into your heart a mass of refuse matter? Observe,
then, the cause of the wicked thoughts which come
to you on your knees in prayer ; the manifestation
of the devil, the injection of the spawn of hell. In
the sixth chapter of Ephesians, it is said : "Above
all, taking the shield of faith, wherewith ye shall be

able to quench all the fiery darts of the wicked."
Fiery darts are an injection of the prince of darkness, and therefore I beg of you, be reminded, God
has given you a shield upon which to quench all
the fiery darts. The shield to which Paul refers,
was a piece of defensive armor, about seven feet in
height. I could stand under one of those shields.
Suppose enemies were shooting at me with their
arrows, it would be wisdom in me to get under my
shield. The shield is not an aggressive kind of
armor, but defensive. It is written, "His truth
shall be thy shield and buckler ;" and behind that,
you may quench the fiery darts of the wicked.

A friend once said to me, "It is not so much the
evil thoughts that come to you ; the danger is when
you say, ' Here, my friend, take a chair.'" He is
quite right about it ; it is not the coming of evil
thoughts, but the retention of them. If I were
visiting you, and a thief should break into your
house, and I caught him, I should not speak as
though he were a welcome guest, but I should put
him out. So if evil thoughts come, put them out,
and I don't care if you use a bit of violence. A
man in my country, who had been converted from
a prize fighter, was conducting a meeting, and one
of his old friends came in, and began talking to
annoy him. At last he said, "If you don't keep
quiet, I'll put you out." But the man, thinking he
would do nothing there, kept on, and my friend
came down from the platform and hit him a tremen-
dous blow, and put him out. When remonstrated
with for doing so, he was told that "Vengeance is

Mine, saith the Lord." " I know it," said he, "I was only helping Him a bit." I would not have you imitate any acts of unkindness, but to be wise as serpents, and harmless as doves.

Many of us have not looked on the face of Christ, but the best thing that could be done has been done. He has written a series of letters—so faithful, so full! and these letters contain His mind. He has sent us this Book, which is. the mind of Christ, written out in its beautiful details for us, and we possess this, we feed upon it. May we know what it is to be alive unto God through Jesus Christ our Lord, and when men turn away from God's great treasury to the things of time and sense, we pity them and sorrow over them in our hearts.

Instead of so much of the *Tribune*, why not the glorious testimony that eomes from Thy tribunal— from the loving presence of the living God ? Why not the *Herald* of God's testimony ? Why not the *Sun* of righteousness? God help you to understand how God hath eondeseended to be a letter-writer. He has described, and behind the invention of the printing press, He has given to us the traces of His glorious thought! Anticipate the time when we shall be like Him ; and let the interim be filled with the glorious Word of our Master. And if you want to know God's letters, ask Him concerning them ; don't read them second-hand.

God bless to you these testimonies of His truth. May you learn His blessed Word, till you can say, " Not I, but Christ liveth in me."

CHRIST LIFTED UP.

JOHN XII. 32.

AND I, IF I BE LIFTED UP FROM THE EARTH, WILL DRAW ALL
MEN UNTO ME.

THESE words of the Lord Jesus form a part of the conversation that fell from His lips, when certain Greeks came to Philip, and said, "Sir, we would see Jesus." And Jesus answered in these words,—they do not appear to have necessarily any connection with the question put,— "Except a corn of wheat fall into the ground and die, it abideth alone : but if it die, it bringeth forth much fruit." Now these words have reference to this great fact, that the Lord Jesus Christ, who is incorruptible seed, came into the world to die for our sins, and to rise again for our salvation. It is written, "God hath given to us eternal life, and this life is in His Son. He that hath the Son hath life: and He that hath not the Son of God hath not life."

Jesus declared: "I, if I be lifted up from the earth, will draw all men unto Me." And now, I

wish to call your attention to the lifting up of
Jesus. A 'lifting Him up,' is to declare the same
sentiment to the world — God's great love ; " For
God so loved the world, that He gave His only
begotten Son, that whosoever believeth in Him
should not perish, but have everlasting life. For
God sent not His Son into the world to condemn
the world ; but that the world through Him might
be saved." But as man is everywhere a sinner,
how are sinners to be saved ? Jesus Christ answers
this question : " For Christ also hath once suffered
for sins, the just for the unjust." He said, " I have
a baptism to be baptized with ; and how am I
straitened till it be accomplished ! " The great
work of Jesus Christ on earth was *to die*, however
important His life ; however blessed it may be for
us to recognize that the righteousness of Christ
comes by imputation, that His personal integrity
blesses us who believe in Him ; however blessed to
see His life, His hands full with blessings everywhere, healing the leper, cleansing from sin and
guilt and defilement, giving sight to the blind,
raising the dead, turning men from darkness unto
light ;—however blessed all these, yet this is but a
minor part of Christ's work. The great work of
Christ in the world was to be the sacrifice for sin ;
to deal with sin, that cost the death of Christ, for it
is written : " Once in the end of the world hath
He appeared to put away sin by the sacrifice of
Himself," and thank God, He *has* put away sin.

Next observe, that the Lord Jesus Christ has
been lifted up in order to demonstrate, that the

work of salvation has been accomplished by Him ;
He did not undertake a work that He failed in.
To-day God sits over all blessed forever, because
He dealt successfully with every foe to man ; He
dealt successfully with sin, to bring to an end the
corrupt life that you and I have, as related to
Adam ; for the cause of the death of Christ, or
rather, the issue of His death, was this, that He
brought to an end a sinful life. I say, that as
surely as Christ died for me, my relationship to
Adam is at an end ; my condition as a sinner is a
thing of the past ; not now related to condemnation ; not now under the law. I know that, because
Christ was lifted up on the cross more than eighteen
hundred years ago ; I know by that work of His
alone, I am a saved man. I am not saved by my
faith ; not because I pray ; not because I am one
whit better than you, but because on the cross
Jesus put away my sin, as far as the east is from
the west ; and I lift up Jesus, in order that you may
go out of this house believing Him for yourselves.

If you have never pleaded death in Christ before,
plead it now. If you have been on the wrong
track for years, remember that the law demands of
you the forfeiture of your life on account of sin.
If I were a felon, having broken the laws of the
Commonwealth, the law would not say, ' Sir, you
must be a better man ;' the law would demand its
penalty, and I should be punished ; and the penalty
of sin is death, and either the penalty of your sin
shall rest on Him, or, by your voluntary unbelief,
it rests on you. God in Christ reconciled the world

unto Himself, and unto you He has imputed the work of reconciliation, and I bring to you God's ministry of reconciliation, — " He that believeth on Him is not condemned." I lift Him up, and call you to behold this Blessed One.

" See from His head, His hands, His feet,
Sorrow and love flow mingled down."

I lift up to you a risen Christ ; not now dead, but risen from the dead, and I ask you to believe in Jesus Christ as your life.

It is as though this body of mine, on account of my sins, had forfeited life, and I were lying upon this platform a corpse. My old life is at an end, and the eternal God draws near and infuses into this frame of mine, a new life, Christ Jesus in me. How many have yet to master this simplest proposition in the works of God? " I am crucified with Christ," said Paul ; I hung with Him upon the cross ; I was delivered with Him to death ; in the Greek it is "co-crucified." We have a partnership with Him, and not only were we crucified with Christ, we may say also with the Apostle, " Nevertheless I live ; yet not I, but Christ liveth in me." And I would have you realize this consciousness of the Christ-life within you. Some of you are conscious enough of what is meant by human life, and how many thoughts come springing up as we think of what life is—power, friendship, joy, sorrow, companionship. Oh, what a word is *life!* But in contradistinction with the life of Christ, it is a poor little thing.

9*

I thank God, that Christ nestles in this heart;
He is omnipotent and omnipresent. Do you ask
how God can dwell in you? Christ can make
Himself infinitely little: " His name shall be called
Wonderful, Counsellor, The mighty God, The everlasting Father, The Prince of Peace." " Not I, but
Christ liveth in me," is the anthem and song of
my daily life. And I say to every one here, that
Christ offers you a life as infinitely above everything Adam possessed before He fell, as Christ is
superior to Adam ; a life of eternal progression, of
mighty development and boundless energy. God's
power works in me mightily when I need it, and
again is as quiet as a babe on its mother's breast.
This beautiful life of dignity and ease and power,
the life that Abraham possessed ; the life that
Isaiah possessed ; that Ezekiel, Paul, Peter and
John possessed : that I have, that you may have.
If Christ is lifted up in your heart, Jesus Christ
draws you unto Himself. You may boast that you
are alive ; we who believe in God boast that we
are dead. Let a farmer keep the seed in his barn,
and what of the crop next fall ? And thus the man
who refuses to die, refuses the gospel.

This life is God's gift. See the woman coming
out from Sychar, a city of Samaria, to the well ;
between desire and satiety in constant motion,—
a fitting type of human character, desire on one
hand, satiety on the other ; but she comes in contact with the Son of God, and He tells her: " If
thou knewest the gift of God, * * * thou wouldst
have asked of Him, and He would have given thee

living water. The woman saith unto Him, * * *
From whence then hast Thou that living water?
* * * Jesus answered and said unto her, * * *
Whosoever drinketh of the water that I shall give
him shall never thirst ; but the water that I shall
give him shall be in him a well of water springing
up into everlasting life. The woman saith unto
Him, Sir, give me this water, that I thirst not,
neither come hither to draw." She was an adulteress. I say this, because I am constantly meeting this difficulty. If there be a drunkard before
me, he is as welcome as though his heart was
broken for his sin. My friends, we must not have
any hedges about God's well of living water ; we
must not have it fenced up, so as to keep people
outside. What we want is the living Christ. If a
man were delirious with fever, would you say,
" He is too bad for a physician ! Wait till the
crisis has passed, and then call a physician." What
a delusion ! and yet, that is the gospel that some
are preaching ; — a man must make himself better,
then there is salvation for him !

What does God say to the adulteress ? She
asked and received God's gift of the living Christ,
and the gift changed her completely, and her heart
was purged of its sin, — God's workmanship new-
fashioned ; and she went into Sychar a preacher of
the gospel, saying, "Come, see a man which told
me all things that ever I did : is not this the
Christ ? " Christ is mighty to save, and I pray He
will draw you to Him by the cords of His love, by
the testimony of His Word, by a thousand influ-

ences; but I solemnly and affectionately charge and
plead with you, do not resist the drawing of Christ.
A London minister said, that God never went
behind any man and pushed him to the cross. He
never will ; *He draws* by truth, by affection. And
here let me beg of you, be not self-willed, be not
doggedly set in your way. As Christ said unto the
Jews, "Ye will not come to Me, that ye might
have life."

If you will not believe in Christ, then He will
draw you to Him, — for no one can escape the
drawing of Christ, — but alas! alas! He draws you
for judgment. Yesterday morning I came in contact with two young men, who had been out in the
filthiness of a New York night of debauch. Poor
fellows, the mark of the animal was there, and I
thought, if this is the outside, what must the inside
be. Why does Christ produce such work as that?
And yet I have seen thousands of men who think it
manly to be without Christ. I thank God for the
drawing power of Jesus Christ, and whilst I deprecate the loss of souls, ye who reject Christ, when
He comes to judge all men, will also be rejected. ' I
called and ye refused ; ye were deaf to My voice.'
Oh, brethren, I charge you, reject not the drawing
of Jesus Christ! He is drawing you by the cords
of His love. Come now to Jesus, and let His
beautiful life flood your being, that you may say:
' Not I, but Christ dwelleth in me.' From this
hour let your winter be over and gone, and Christ
dwell in you. Be not longer the slaves of sin, but
the children of Jesus Christ. If the Son shall

make you free, you shall be free indeed ; free from
self-will, free from dogged obstinacy.

A man of understanding who knows not Christ,
is like the beast that perisheth. Arouse, men, and
see that the life of Christ is easy to live. It is an
easy thing to do right when we live in Christ ; it is
a hard thing to do wrong when a man has Christ :
but alas, thousands of Christians are wedded to
little better than a theory, — a mere matter of so
many sermons and prayers. Thank God, we dwell
with Him, He is our head. He did not invite you,
to forsake you. "I, if I be lifted up, will draw all
men unto Me." Grasp that thought, God dwells in
us and we in Him. It is a grand thing to have a
life we cannot lose ; a great thing to have a life co-
equal to the duration of eternity in perpetuity ; a
great thing to have a life which death cannot destroy ; a great thing to have a life which, when
temptations are before it, says "No." Will any of
you say, 'I take Him as God's gift. He is mine. I
receive Him now, for God's gift is free.' I would
that every one of you would say, I know the life in
Christ, I am ' always bearing about in the body the
dying of Jesus Christ, that the life also of Jesus
might be made manifest in my body ;' for our life is
always delivered unto death, and Christ died that
the life also of Jesus might be made manifest in
our flesh.

I am bound to tell you how satisfied I am with
the life of Christ. I thank God for it. It is a life
glorious to possess. "I am come that they might
have life, and that they might have it more abun-

dantly:" a life that goes on in endless progression for ever and ever. This is the gospel; what a glorious theme. I am not insensible to the important place commerce occupies, but in view of eternal salvation, it sinks out of sight. I came here, not to preach a system, but Christ. Some of you have been living in self; get out of self and live in Christ. Put off the old man which is corrupt, and put on the new man. Suppose I had a fine picture, and a wretched daub, do you think I would spend my time looking at that thing, and touching it up here and there, trying to improve it? Some of you have been patching up your old self; it is crucifixion and death and burial that it needs. Take in the glory of this, God's Christ in us. I don't want any other light. I would say, as Martin Luther said, "If any man knock at my heart, and ask who liveth here, I shall say, not Martin Luther, but Jesus Christ." Such is the gospel, and would I could leave with you this great joy. " Unto Him that loved us, and washed us from our sins in His own blood, and hath made us kings and priests unto God and His Father; to Him be glory and dominion for ever and ever. AMEN."

THE UNJUST STEWARD

━━━oo°∘°oo━━━

THE portion of God's Word to which I desire now to call your attention, is the deeply instructive parable of the Unjust Steward; and before remarking upon it, I will ask you to turn with me to the sixteenth chapter of St. Luke's Gospel, and let us read it :—

And He said also unto His disciples, There was a certain rich man, which had a steward; and the same was accused unto him that he had wasted his goods. And he called him, and said unto him, How is it that I hear this of thee? give an account of thy stewardship; for thou mayest be no longer steward.

Then the steward said within himself, What shall I do? for my lord taketh away from me the stewardship: I cannot dig; to beg I am ashamed. I am resolved what to do, that, when I am put out of the stewardship, they may receive me into their houses.

So he called every one of his lord's debtors unto him, and said unto the first, How much owest thou unto my lord? And he said, A hundred measures of oil. And he said unto him, Take thy bill, and sit down quickly, and write fifty. Then said he to another, And how much

owest thou? And he said, A hundred measures of wheat.
And he said unto him, Take thy bill, and write fourscore.
And the lord commended the unjust steward, because he
had done wisely : for the children of this world are in
their generation wiser than the children of light.

And I say unto you, Make to yourselves friends of the
mammon of unrighteousness ; that, when ye fail, they
may receive you into everlasting habitations.   He that is
faithful in that which is least is faithful also in much :
and he that is unjust in the least is unjust also in much.
If therefore ye have not been faithful in the unrighteous
mammon, who will commit to your trust the true riches?
And if ye have not been faithful in that which is another
man's, who shall give you that which is your own ?

I wish you to note the principal things given to
us in the verses which I have read.   First, we have
a certain rich man who had a steward.   The steward is unfortunate and wastes his lord's goods ;
therefore the lord commands him to appear before
him and give an account of his stewardship.   The
steward fears he will be put out of his stewardship ;
the best course to pursue under the circumstances,
is what is just now occupying his mind.   He does
not appear to have robbed his master, but he had
. wasted his goods.   So he determined he would
make his master's debtors accomplices to some
extent with himself.   And he called them together
and said, to one and to another, How much owest
thou to my master ?   These two examples are only
a few of the many.

How artful it is, the way he acts.   He says to
this one, Take thy bill and sit down quickly and

write fifty; to the other, Write fourscore. Notice,
that it is all in the handwriting of the men themselves, so that they were silenced. Very clever he
was, — he was a very shrewd thief, — he did it well.
His lord found it out and commended the steward ;
but you are not to suppose it was the Lord Jesus
Christ.

So far the history concerns the steward ; but from
this point the Lord Jesus takes hold, as He so
often does in human affairs. He says, The children
of this world are in their generation wiser than the
children of light. Oh, what a melancholy truth
that is. Take business men ; what activity and
energy they display ; take it in any department
you please, the world is right up to the mark in all
things. But alas! alas! this is not so with the
children of God. The children of the world are in
their generation wiser than the children of light.
Let me ask you to find occasion in your spiritual
life to be as energetic as you are in your business
life. Are you as really anxious about the health of
your soul, as you make it your earnest study that
your body shall be strong? If you have any bodily
affliction, you want to be restored. I remind you
that God desires above all things, that we have
spiritual prosperity : are you careful about your
soul's spiritual health? Are you striving in watchful prayerfulness?' Do you realize that you are
living not for time, but for eternity? not for the
world, but for heaven ; not for pleasure, but to
shine forth His praise, who hath called you out of
the darkness into the light. Instead of the Chris-

tian life we should be living, how many Christians
are living a life that is a poor dwarfed thing. Not
only is this the case in reference to our personal
experience, but it is true of those engaged in the
work of Christ.

Sunday School Teachers, are you as attentive in
your Sunday School as you are in your business?
We have Sunday School twice a day, and the books
show that the attendance of teachers in the afternoon is about half of that in the morning. When
would you dare treat an earthly employer like that?
Suppose you said to your employer, 'Well, it was
damp this morning, and I had not my umbrella, and
I thought that I would not come to work.' I
verily believe that the devil seems to comb some
people down smoothly after their regeneration.
And mark the solemn reproof for this, "The children of this world are in their generation wiser
than the children of light."

Now notice, "And I say unto you, Make to yourselves friends of the mammon of unrighteousness."
What is meant by this? I see, for example, a
worldly man, of power and education and riches; a
man of business; a man who uses all these powers
well, and makes them tell among his fellow men.
If he has attained a certain political position, he
says, Higher — "Excelsior!" And so the idea of
progress is always before the earnest spirit of a
man who is looking after some higher attainment.
Thank God, there are many who possess a great
amount of stock in trade. God has given to you,
perhaps, a gift of speech. Well, use it for Him.

Again, some of you possess money. I beg of you, let that money be expended for Christ. Money may be turned into ships and bread and missionary enterprises.

Christ says : — " Make to yourselves friends of the mammon of unrighteousness ; that, when ye fail, they may receive you into everlasting habitations." I dare say, some of you have been puzzled about the meaning of this. I tell you, I believe it means you and I are regenerated when we are taken out of the world. Turn to the first chapter of the epistle of Galatians, fourth verse. Speaking of the work of Christ's apostles, it says : " Who gave Himself for our sins, that He might deliver us from this present evil world, according to the will of God and our Father." Now, every believer in Christ is delivered from this present evil world. You can say to-day you are not a citizen of New York but of heaven. All your life dates from that centre. You have no right to say that you are a citizen of this world, for it is not true, since He has adopted you into His family and redeemed you. Then let all the issues of your life tend where your life has its source and spring and flow. And when you fail in this world they may " receive you into everlasting habitations,"—it will not be by fraud. How inspiring the thought of the welcome we shall receive from those we have been instrumental in saving. They have died and gone before, and they will receive us into the everlasting habitations.

But the poor worldly soul, while death is feeling at his heart strings,—what account can he render for wasted powers? Oh that men should be such fools, staking existence upon the poor possessions of the present. "Lay not up for yourselves treasures upon earth, where moth and rust doth corrupt and where thieves break through and steal, but lay up for yourselves treasures in heaven, where moth and rust cannot corrupt and where thieves do not break through and steal." And even thus we would have abundant entrance into the everlasting kingdom of Christ. Not as though we had been faithless, but because we have been faithful to Him who shall say, "Well done, thou good and faithful servant, thou hast been faithful over few things, I will make thee ruler over many."

Now turn to the twenty-fifth chapter of Matthew. The close of the chapter gives us the judgment of Christ. Read from the thirty-first verse :—

"When the Son of man shall come in his glory, and all the holy angels with him, then shall he sit upon the throne of his glory : and before him shall be gathered all nations : and he shall separate them one from another, as a shepherd divideth his sheep from the goats : and he shall set the sheep on his right hand, but the goats on the left. Then shall the King say unto them on his right hand, Come, ye blessed of my Father, inherit the kingdom prepared for you from the foundation of the world."

Particularly notice the next verses :—

"For I was a hungered, and ye gave me meat : I was thirsty, and ye gave me drink : I was a stranger, and ye took me in : naked, and ye clothed me : I was sick, and ye visited me : I was in prison, and ye came unto me.

Then shall the righteous answer him, saying, Lord, when saw we thee a hungered, and fed thee? or thirsty, and gave thee drink? When saw we thee a stranger, and took thee in? or naked, and clothed thee? Or when saw we thee sick, or in prison, and came unto thee? And the King shall answer and say unto them, Verily I say unto you, Inasmuch as ye have done it unto one of the least of these my brethren, ye have done it unto me."

Now notice the personal pronouns through the whole judgment. He refers to Himself :—

"Then shall he say also unto them on the left hand, Depart from me, ye cursed, into everlasting fire, prepared for the devil and his angels : For I was a hungered, and ye gave me no meat : I was thirsty, and ye gave me no drink : I was a stranger, and ye took me not in : naked, and ye clothed me not : sick, and in prison, and ye visited me not.

Then shall they also answer him, saying, Lord, when saw we thee a hungered, or athirst, or a stranger, or naked, or sick, or in prison, and did not minister unto thee? Then shall he answer them, saying, Verily I say unto you, Inasmuch as ye did it not to one of the least of these, ye did it not to me.

And these shall go away into everlasting punishment : but the righteous into life eternal."

How any man dares to trifle with the truth in the face of the eternal doom of the wicked, I am at a loss to understand. Christ says in the final tribunal, "These shall go away into everlasting punishment and these into life eternal."

I pray you keep to these words; they are your
strength and salvation, and you have no time to
lose. Are you in the habit of visiting the prisons
in your city? Are you in business for Christ?
Are you making your profession of Christianity,
child's play? Are you wont to make your business
contribute to the glory of God? Did you ever
notice that verse in the book of Titus, "Put them
in mind to be subject to principalities and powers,
to obey magistrates, to be ready to every good
work." How many Christians there are in business which does not honor their God. I could not
imagine a man having to do with distilleries or rum
shops, and calling himself a Christian. I tell you
until we get the gospel of Christ into practical
works, men will not believe we are really Christians.
You, perhaps, may tell me I can make fifty thousand
dollars. What is that to me? I was not redeemed
to make money. In the south of England I came
in contact with a man who was a brewer and a
leading officer in a church; he wanted me to come
and dwell with him. I wrote and said, "Has Christ
to say of you, that you are a leading officer in the
church and yet the greatest Sabbath breaker in
Dover? Did God redeem you to open the door,
Sunday after Sunday, inviting working men away
from their homes? Do you say to alter your course
would cost you half your fortune? Let it go!" I
told him I would rather come and share a crust
with him in a lowly cottage, than dwell with him in
splendor, secured by such means. Oh, my friends,
I ask you to be careful that to you it may be said

by the great Master, "Thou hast been faithful over
a few things, I will make thee ruler over many
things." I ask you, brethren, are you faithful in
your own households? I have found it easy to go
upon a platform and make an oratorical display,
and yet when the piece of fireworks is over I am no
stronger in Christ, I feel that it is child's play.

I remember praying, Oh, God, just make me
faithful in little things. One Sunday night, after I
had been speaking to about two thousand people,
when I came down the platform steps, a little
fellow standing there said, "I want to talk to you
about Jesus." It was God's answer to my prayer,
and it was a real joy to me to take this little fellow
alone, and speak with him as tenderly and earnestly
as though I had been standing before the crowd
who were listening to me fifteen minutes before.
You and I are in danger of not being faithful in
little things. We have a proverb in England, "If
you take care of the pence, the pounds will take
care of themselves." I verily think the difficulty
is, not to be faithful in large spheres, but to be
constantly with Him in His mighty teachings.
His mightiest lessons were made to individuals. I
entreat you to be faithful. Remember, you have
received from your blessed God, the true riches.
Use what you have, if you have not much. You
may say, perhaps, our place of meeting is a little
one. I am not sorry for that, for most of God's
prosperity comes in the midst of circumstances we
would not choose. Many churches have been
blessed with such a tide of prosperity; the church

may have been small, and in some back street, and a man of wealth comes along and says, "Here you are doing a great work; you ought to be in a better church; I'll start the list," and your efforts after that are all centered on getting the wretched money, and when it is finished and you are in your new church, you might have written "Ichabod" on the spiritual prosperity of that place. If this appears to be severe, you know it is only exceeded in severity by its truth.

Be faithful to Him, for you have got a grand opportunity. Let us give our eyes to Him, that He may weep over sinners; give Him our hands, that He may yearn over sinners. I beseech you, see to it that you walk with Him in the beautiful surrender of an undivided heart. There is a word the French use a great deal, the word "abandon." I would like to say, abandon yourselves to Christ. If He wants you to speak to one little child, or to thousands, don't hold up a finger to tell which it shall be.

I want to impress this thought upon you, that you have *the opportunity*. If the angels in heaven had your opportunity, not one would be in heaven in a quarter of an hour. As we leave off here, we shall begin in the world to come. Oh, that we may not only know what it is to be in possession of the true riches, but to use them; may we strive to use the powers God has given us. This is a life of perfect freedom. Be a man in the fight. Be a hero in the strife! Shall we be laggards in the race? Oh, stand firm, acquit ye like men. We are called to as glorious a service as it is possible for the human mind to contain, and Christ stands ready to say to us, "Well done, thou good and faithful servant: thou hast been faithful over a few things, I will make thee ruler over many things." Be faithful to Him, if you want an increase of faith. Use what thou hast, and thy Master shall develop, and God shall stand ready to receive you into His presence with His, "Well done," and ye shall say, "Not unto us." The Lord bless these thoughts to each one of you.

THE SEVENTH OF ROMANS.

THE seventh chapter of Romans is my theme to-day, and first of all, I desire you to note the brief statement that I make of the argument of the apostle in this experience. In the first chapter, we have God's testimony concerning the condition of the whole heathen world. In the second chapter, we have God's testimony concerning Israel. The chapters differ in that great distinction, that God gave His verdict on the world without revelation ; then to that people that hath its rise in Abraham, the friend of God. And God testifies alike concerning man without revelation and Israel with revelation. He said, they are alike and altogether corrupt. Hence, in the third chapter, we read, the whole world is guilty before God. Look at this chapter, nineteenth verse, " Now we know that what things soever the law saith, it saith to them who are under the law : that every mouth may be stopped, and all the world may become guilty before God." Every mouth and all the world ; not merely the world as such, but the entire human

family, 'every mouth and all the world;' "therefore by the deeds of the law there shall no flesh be
justified in His sight: for by the law is the knowledge of sin. But now the righteousness of God
without the law is manifested, being witnessed by
the law and the prophets ; even the righteousness
of God which is by faith of Jesus Christ unto all
them that believe." Mark that word ; let me emphasize it ; *upon all that believe.*

In the fourth chapter, we have demonstrated two
characters which, in the past history of the world,
illustrate the principle just laid down. One is
Abraham, the other is David. Abraham believes
on God, and it is accounted unto him for righteousness. And David is the man of whom it is said,
' Blessed is the man to whom God imputeth righteousness without works.' I pray you, give up the
labor of trying to be worthy by your works, for
there is no difference, all have sin. At the close
of the fourth chapter, we learn that "it was not
written for his sake alone, that it was imputed to
him ; but for us also, to whom it shall be imputed,
if we believe on Him that raised up Jesus our Lord
from the dead ; who was delivered for our offences,
and was raised again for our justification." In the
fifth chapter, we are justified by faith, and therefore, being justified, "we have peace with God
through our Lord Jesus Christ." And so it enlarges
upon the blessedness of the condition into which
faith brings us, till we read at the close of the
chapter, " Moreover the law entered, that the offence might abound. But where sin abounded,

grace did much more abound." The law is like the probing-knife of the physician, it discovers the disease of sin.

The argument is carried on from the fifth to the end of the eighth chapter ; the sixth and seventh are a kind of parenthesis. And we read in the eighth chapter :

There is therefore now no condemnation to them which are in Christ Jesus, who walk not after the flesh, but after the Spirit. For the law of the Spirit of life in Christ Jesus hath made me free from the law of sin and death. For what the law could not do, in that it was weak through the flesh, God sending his own Son in the likeness of sinful flesh, and for sin, condemned sin in the flesh.

What can we do ? The law cannot justify transgressions ; it must condemn them. What the law could not do, God sent His own Son in the likeness of sinful flesh to do. He judged and condemned and punished sin.

Now, I want you to remember, that the apostle in these chapters, sixth and seventh, first of all shows us what our position is. In the sixth chapter and third verse, " Know ye not, that so many of us as were baptized into Jesus Christ were baptized into His death ? " That is, we have fellowship in death ; we are buried with Him, and like as Christ was raised up from the dead, even so we shall walk in newness of life : and shall you bury the Lord Jesus Christ this side of the cross ? If He had not died, then any one would have a right

to come into the same position ; but if He died,
then are you in the same position. If Christ was
buried, then have you been buried. Think seriously of the fact, that you have been delivered to
death in Christ, and as truly as Christ has risen
from the dead, so are you, who believe in Him.
Never think of your former experience, for all that
has past away.

That being the case, look at the seventh chapter
of Romans ; it takes up the argument :

Know ye not, brethren, (for I speak to them that
know the law,) how that the law hath dominion over a
man as long as he liveth? For the woman which hath a
husband is bound by the law to her husband so long as
he liveth ; but if the husband be dead, she is loosed from
the law of her husband. So then if, while her husband
liveth, she be married to another man, she shall be called
an adulteress : but if her husband be dead, she is free
from that law ; so that she is no adulteress, though she
be married to another man.

Observe the illustration ; here a woman is introduced upon the scene. While she is married to a
husband, she has no power to release herself from
the obligation ; law and the husband both hold her ;
but if her husband dies, she is obviously free from
the husband. Notice the fourth verse, " Wherefore,
my brethren, ye also are become dead to the law
by the body of Christ." We never speak about
the body of men till death has supervened. Wherefore ye take into account that the Lord Jesus Christ
was made a curse for us, and by His death delivered

us from the bondage of the law ; by no power possible could we liberate ourselves. The law can demand obedience to all its details and exact its penalties.

Such being the case, the Lord Jesus Christ has come to redeem, and through love He has accomplished His work. "Wherefore, my brethren, ye also are become dead to the law by the body of Christ; that ye should be married to another, even to Him who is raised from the dead, that we should bring forth fruit unto God." To whom are you married? To the Lord? because if so, the apostle says, "When we were in the flesh, the motions of sins, which were by the law, did work in our members to bring forth fruit unto death." We have a great truth contained in this seventh chapter of Romans, that application of the law as a will. It works in our members to bring forth fruit unto death ; it cannot do otherwise, for man is a transgressor. This is so, not because the law is sinful and weak, but you and I are weak ; the law is just and holy, but we are utterly unable to be obedient to the law. Obedient, married to another, for the object of Christ's coming was to bring us away from condemnation into justification. United to the law, it was : " Cursed be every one who continueth not to do them ; " united to Christ, " we have an advocate with the Father." We have not a Lord to condemn, but one who is mighty to save. He says to us, if we think we have no sin, we deceive ourselves, and my faith is that He is faithful and just and will forgive my sins,—faithful and

just to forgive us our sins, and cleanse us from
all unrighteousness. Such is the result of being
married to Christ. He is not united to us in the
thoughts of condemnation ; not in a legal covenant,
but in a covenant of love, and its culmination, the
glories of heaven.

Now let us carefully proceed. " But now we are
delivered from the law, that being dead wherein we
were held ; that we should serve in newness of
spirit, and not in the oldness of the letter." That
does not mean we are without law, for the apostle
says, " Not without law to God, but under the law
to Christ." Let me give you an illustration. We
as parents do not rule our children by law ; it is a
bond of love between the children and ourselves.
God has tried law, and the law has failed, because
man was a transgressor. God has tried love, and
love casteth out fear. When you know God loves
you perfectly, it will cast out all fear, and we shall
be able to bring Him the outcoming affections
of our hearts, and love to do the will of Him who
loves as God loves.

All through this chapter, observe the absence
of the name of the Lord Jesus Christ till the close ;
there are plenty of pronouns, but no name mentioned, and therefore I think we cannot fail to see
what the apostle is doing ; he is just illustrating
what he said would come, namely, That the law is
applied to the light of long continued experience ;
when I speak about this passage, do not suppose
I agree with those who say that this is a description of Paul's experience, still in a legal condition.

It shows us God's interpretation, that if the law be applied, such is the law that it cannot but work in the direction of condemnation to us.

Notice what follows: "Is the law sin? God forbid." Nothing could allow such a thought. "Nay, I had not known sin, but by the law: for I had not known lust, except the law had said, Thou shalt not covet. But sin, taking occasion by the commandment, wrought in me all manner of concupiscence. For without the law sin was dead. For I was alive without the law once: but when the commandment came, sin revived and I died." I want you to see the beauty of that. I was alive without law once, but directly law came with its power, in testimony of God's holiness, — God will by no means clear the guilty, — then my own sinfulness came to light. When I saw this, I was thankful to find my way to the cross. If I were to transgress against the laws of England, the law would punish me; it demands its penalties, and so does God's law. Oh, beloved friends, let me appeal to you solemnly, if there is a soul before me taken up with the idea, that "I am going to be justified by my attempts to keep from sin," I can hear God's sentence confronting your probably fatal mistake. Paul says, 'When the law came, sin revived;' he does not say, 'My attempts to obey,' but, '*Sin* stood up before me, and I died.' He did not escape the penalty; no, he did suffer the penalty of that broken law. This is the object of Christ's coming into the world. This is why we grasp the fact that we are dead with Him. However misunderstood by others, the believer in Christ knows it is his song of gladness. I wonld rather hold that one guarantee of not being condemned in the days to come, than to boast as Paul boasted, that touching the law as God gave it, he is blameless. The believer in Christ boasts that he is dead with Christ.

Notice, " The commandment, which was ordained to life." I don't think the commandment was ordained to life in the sense generally understood. The law was to be our school-master to bring us unto Jesus ; to show us our sinfulness and need of a Saviour ; and then the apostle says, " I found to be unto death. For sin, taking occasion by the commandment, deceived me, and by it slew me." How this man comes back to the place of death ; no matter what part of his experience he refers to, he seems to rush back to his sense of his death in Christ as quickly as he can : —

Wherefore the law is holy, and the commandment holy, and just, and good. Was then that which is good made death unto me? God forbid. But sin, that it might appear sin, working death in me by that which is good ; that sin by the commandment might become exceeding sinful.

And to-day, I take it there is not one of us who has walked with God in the light, — let me say, we are all called to walk in the light, it is in the light that the discovery of sin is made ; perhaps some of us may go out in the sunshine and find our garments not so good as we thought them ; it is

10*

not because they are not so good, only because we
are in the light ; as we walk with God in the light,
the discovery of sin must ensue.

I am not surprised that Paul says, "This is a
faithful saying, and worthy of all acceptation, that
Christ Jesus came into the world to save sinners ;
of whom I am chief." He said this just before his
death. It is a blessed thing to have a deep sense
of the power of sin. I would that all of you had a
deeper detestation of sin. Sometimes I have heard
it remarked, that in consequence of the teachings
of friends with whom I am associated, I have been
spoken of as though I believed I was without sin.
Believe me, I have no character to lose, I gave it
to God long ago ; but I say that I mourn deeply,
that any should ever have such low thoughts of sin.
Sin to me is not what I am conscious of, sins that
I don't know ; for I would not make my consciousness the gauge of what sin is. Shall children of
the loving God say they are without sin ? No.

Sin, to some people, is merely a kind of negative
thing. I will tell you how I regard righteousness.
Suppose I see a tree full of corrupt fruit ; though I
take every particle of fruit from the tree, I don't
make it a good tree. You think if you cease from
sin, you are sinless ! What a horrid delusion !
Our consciousness is not the measure of sin, for
one-third of the Jewish sacrifices were for the sins
of ignorance. *Ceasing from sin is not righteousness !* More than this, if there were no positive sin
attached to you, that would not make you righteous.
The nature of the tree must be changed. There

you have God's idea of righteousness. That which troubles me is not the commission of actual transgression, but I mourn when I think how little fruit I bring to Him who redeemed us. God arouse you all, to know what sin is, for as you grow into a hatred of sin, and you love the law,—for the law is holy,—I am bound to say with David, that though it condemns me, I pronounce it good and love it. As you grow in increasing fellowship with God, it brings out the evil, till sin shall be loathsome, — till you turn away from self and sin to look fully on Him who is our righteousness and our life. " For we know that the law is spiritual : but I am carnal, sold under sin." The apostle is now speaking of his new nature, the Christ-life and the old one, and they war against each other. We have a proverb, that "nature abhors a vacuum," and I can say, that is true of grace. If we want to know most of the Christ-life and least of the energy of the flesh, then we must be sure we possess the life of Christ, that will enable us to keep our foot on the neck of evil.

Let us cleanse ourselves from all sinfulness. Is this compatible with an increase of the sense of sin ? Remember in the sixth chapter of Isaiah, how the glory of Jehovah caused the prophet to say, " Woe is me ! for I am undone ; because I am a man of unclean lips, and I dwell in the midst of a people of unclean lips." He is speaking of his past experience. There is a diversity of opinion as to what Paul meant in the next few verses. He must have referred either to past experience or an exceptional case. If you will grant me that it was an exceptional thing in the apostle's history, then I go with you; but if you want to make out it was a common thing for him to be troubled, I cannot allow that. I don't find it a difficult thing to do right, and could not understand being made a partaker of the divine nature, and not liking to do right. Let us be careful here. If any one of us as God's children commit sin, is it not true that we find ourselves confronted by the accusations of conscience? It is not possible that the divine life should be a failure; that partaking of the divine nature should not give victory.

Now notice: "If then I do that which I would not, I consent unto the law that it is good. Now then it is no more I that do it, but sin that dwelleth in me. For I know that in me, (that is, in my flesh,) dwelleth no good thing: for to will is present with me; but how to perform that which is good I find not." There you see is the "I," not the Christ-life, for the apostle distinctly says, "I know that in me dwelleth no good thing, for to will is present with me, but how to perform that which is good, I find not. For the good that I would I do not, but the evil which I would not, that I do. Now if I do that which I would not, it is no more I that do it, but sin that dwelleth in me." We must be careful here; St. Paul does not mean to affirm that he is not guilty when he does what he would not. It is the old nature, but sin, all the same.

My friends, let us be honest with ourselves. Take temper; you have no more right to lose your temper than to be a thief. Some may say, temper is an infirmity. If you could be put in prison for twenty-four hours for losing temper, you would soon find it was not an infirmity. It is a wretched sin. For years I hindered my business by the manifestation of a hasty temper; one never says the right thing in that condition. I became so disgusted with myself, that I determined to put the whole thing into the hands of the Lord, and I never shall forget the definiteness with which I told Him, "Lord, I am utterly powerless, take me in hand." And the Lord has kept it down, so that I have not seen its manifestation for years. I am sure grace will make us strongest in the weakest points of our character. I find always a recognition of the two lives, the old and new, the Christ-life and the Saul-of-Tarsus-life; and often we shall find the old life coming up, if we do not watch it. There are mighty forces for evil within us, but there is also One force which is almighty; there are mighty forces without, but there is One who is mightier than them all, — and if we dwell in Him and He in us, that Almighty power will take our part always.

But, continues St. Paul, "I see another law in my members, warring against the law of my mind, and bringing me into captivity to the law of sin which is in my members. O wretched man that I am! who shall deliver me from the body of this death?" Well, some say, 'This brings us to the position we maintained; we have struggled with sin, and we must bear the battle and defeat, till the body of sin is laid down in death.' I used to think so, but I don't now. I thank God, it is not failure but victory.

Take the next verse in connection with it. "O
wretched man that I am! who shall deliver me from
the body of this death! I thank God through
Jesus Christ our Lord. So then with the mind I
myself serve the law of God; but with the flesh the
law of sin." It is a song of triumph. I grant you,
it is a conflict; but it is not conflict and defeat; it
is conflict and victory! "I thank God!" What
for? that sin oppresses? No,—that we have the
victory. Oh brethren, let us realize how indeed
Christ liveth in us. There was a time when I used
to think God had been merciful to me in putting
away my sins, and that I must be exceedingly careful; as though God had put me in some errand
boy's position, and I must work my way up. I
thank God, I have got out of that. God gives us a
fortune; he don't make us errand boys. He gives
us the beautiful, dignified life of Christ Jesus at
once. "So then with the mind I myself serve the
law of God; but with the flesh the law of sin."
Yes, blessed be God, the law of God we want to
know what it is. We love it; but we shall turn
away from that law to the shelter of the loving
Saviour, by whom we live; who came not to curse,
but to bless; not to make us guilty, but innocent.
O wicked man that I am! Yes, when I think of
myself; yes, until the gospel teaches the triumphant anthem: "Thanks be to God, which giveth
us the victory through our Lord Jesus Christ."

THE EPISTLE TO THE HEBREWS.

———◦◦◦◦◦———

MY Dear Friends, I am going this afternoon to speak to you from Paul's Epistle to the Hebrews. The Lord Jesus Christ is the great metropolis of the Book of God. We have over our Royal Exchange in London these words : "The earth is the Lord's and the fullness thereof." And I think we could not have a better thought as the heading of the book of Hebrews than this : "It pleased the Father that in Him should all fullness dwell." If I were asked to write one word across every page of the book of Hebrews, I would write C-H-R-I-S-T.

Now the first chapter :

"God, who at sundry times and in divers manners spake in time past unto the fathers by the prophets, hath in these last days spoken unto us by his Son, whom he hath appointed heir of all things, by whom also he made the worlds ; who being the brightness of his glory, and the express image of his person, and upholding all things by the word of his power, when he had by himself purged our sins, sat down on the right hand of the Majesty on high."

Here is a distinct statement of the creation of the world by the Lord Jesus Christ; that He is the mighty Creator.   From the formation of all created things, the apostle passes to the great fact, that He is the brightness of the Father's glory and the express image of His person.   The words, "express image," are suggested by the mould in which a coin is struck, — the die.   Just so, Jesus Christ is the express image of the person of the Father.   And mark, " Upholding all things by the word of His power."   There is the present eternal power of the Christ of God.   His hand upholds yonder sun; His hand directs the shining stars ; His hand sustains this world in which we dwell.

And then, " when He had by Himself purged our sins," so that, though they might nail both hands to the cross in putting away our sins, yet, when He hung there, He was mighty enough to uphold all things.   Nevertheless, " when He had by Himself purged our sins, sat down on the right hand of the Majesty on high."   The sweet thought suggested, is of a commander who has put to rout every enemy on the field, and now rests from the conflict.

" Being made so much better than the angels, as he hath by inheritance obtained a more excellent name than they."

Here is the platform cleared by the apostle for Christ alone.   Now, as his argument proceeds, he contrasts Christ with the greatest form of created power we know, the angels ; and he says in the subsequent verse, that the Lord Jesus Christ is infinitely superior to them. And observe :

"Unto which of the angels said he at any time, Thou art my Son, this day have I begotten thee? And again, I will be to him a Father, and he shall be to me a Son ? And again, when he bringeth in the first begotten into the world, he saith, And let all the angels of God worship him. And of the angels he saith, Who maketh his angels spirits, and his ministers a flame of fire."

Mark what the Father says to the Son :

"Thy throne, O God, is for ever and ever : a sceptre of righteousness is the sceptre of thy kingdom. Thou hast loved righteousness and hated iniquity."

That is God's ideal character,—"Thou hast loved righteousness and hated iniquity." The world's ideal character is of a man who does not love righteousness too much. Now God's ideal is, "Thou hast loved righteousness, and hated iniquity; therefore God, even thy God, hath anointed thee with the oil of gladness above thy fellows."

"And, Thou, Lord, in the beginning hast laid the foundation of the earth ; and the heavens are the works of thine hands. They shall perish, but thou remainest."

Many of the most magnificent of earthly structures have survived their builders, but here the builder survives.

"They all shall wax old as doth a garment ; and as a vesture shalt thou fold them up, and they shall be changed : but thou art the same, and thy years shall not

fail. But to which of the angels said he at any time,
Sit on my right hand, until I make thine enemies thy
footstool? Are they not all ministering spirits, sent forth
to minister for them who shall be heirs of salvation?"

Thus in the first chapter, the apostle shows us
Christ as the Creator of all things ; angels subject
to Him, and the Son exalted by the Father to the
highest point of regal power. Now, then, in the
second chapter, says the apostle:

"We ought to give the more earnest heed to the
things which we have heard, lest at any time we should
let them slip. For if the word spoken by angels was
steadfast, and every transgression and disobedience received a just recompense of reward ; how shall we escape,
if we neglect so great salvation."

Now, observe, man is here introduced; the object
being to show that man is to be associated with the
Lord Jesus Christ in the glory of the eternal future,
and that is the argument now in this second chapter, and therefore it is *We* who are to give this
earnest heed. Then, referring to the substitution of
the ministry of the Lord Jesus Christ witnessed by
His miracles and power, he saith in the fifth verse,
"Unto the angels hath He not put into subjection
the world to come." Now, angels have been God's
executors in times past, but it is not to angels that
God has put into subjection the world to come, but
to men ; and in order to this, God has stepped from
the divine nature to the human, that He might
raise the human to the divine ; and this was the
purpose of Christ's coming into the world.

"One in a certain place testified, saying, What is man, that thou art mindful of him? or the son of man, that thou visitest him? Thou madest him a little lower than the angels; thou crownedst him with glory and honor, and didst set him over the works of thy hands."

If you and I were to judge of men as we see them now, we should have to say that they are compassed with weakness and infirmities. But by Christ we see that all things are ours. The reason is now stated by the apostle:

"Thou hast put all things in subjection under his feet. For in that he put all in subjection under him, he left nothing that is not put under him. But now we see not yet all things put under him. But we see Jesus, who was made a little lower than the angels for the suffering of death, crowned with glory and honor; that he by the grace of God should taste death for every man. For it became him for whom are all things, and by whom are all things, in bringing many sons unto glory, to make the captain of their salvation perfect through sufferings. For both he that sanctifieth and they who are sanctified are all of one: for which cause he is not ashamed to call them brethren."

I pause to ask, Do you believe this truth, that you are one with Christ? He who sanctifieth is the Lord Jesus Christ, declared to be heir of all things, and we are joint heirs with Christ. I want you to notice how sweetly Jesus says, "I ascend unto My Father, and your Father; and to My God, and your God." If you want to know the fruit of divine love, see it in this relation.

Now, let me ask you to look at the commencement of the third chapter. "Wherefore, holy
brethren, partakers of the heavenly calling,"— do
not ask your consciences whether you are holy:
if I were to appeal to my own feelings, I should
say, "As a man I am a poor sinful creature," but I
hear God say I am a brother in Christ, and I do
not dare to deny His word. "Wherefore, holy
brethren, partakers of the heavenly calling, consider
the Apostle and High Priest of our profession,
Christ Jesus ; who was faithful to Him that appointed Him, as also Moses was faithful in all his
house."

Now, I shall very rapidly pass over three or four
chapters. Here is Moses, who now comes to bear
his meed of testimony to the Lord Jesus Christ.
He is the faithful servant, and now in contrast to
the faithful Son, he leaves the platform to be occupied by Christ alone. Now, under the leadership
of Moses, we have this lesson taught us by Israel:
the heinousness of the sin of unbelief ; and just as
certainly the Holy Ghost stands in our midst, and
warns us that we fall not through unbelief. Observe, now, it is for us to believe. "Said I not
unto thee, that, if thou wouldest believe, thou
shouldest see the glory of God ?" And associated
with Christ, now, I ask you to believe that, one with
Him, all I am going to call your attention to belongs
to us in unison with Himself.

In the beginning of the fourth chapter, you have
Moses' successor. Moses has come and sweetly
spoken of Christ, and left the platform, and now

you have Joshua.   He seems to say, " It was not
myself that I presented to you ; I was but a type
of Jesus, who should lead you into the rest of God."
And now along with Joshua comes the land flowing
with milk and honey.   The land says, " I was but a
type of Christ."   And not only so, but just as you
have the Land and Joshua, you have the Sabbath
spoken of ; Joshua, and the Sabbath and the Land.
They group their testimony to Christ, and leave
the platform to be occupied by Christ alone.   And
then we are told in the twelfth verse, that " The
word of God is quick, and powerful, and sharper
than any two-edged sword, piercing even to the
dividing asunder of soul and spirit, and of the joints
and marrow, and is a discerner of the thoughts and
intents of the heart."

"Seeing then that we have a great high priest, that is
passed into the heavens, Jesus the Son of God, let us
hold fast our profession.   For we have not a high priest
which cannot be touched with the feeling of our infirmities ; but was in all points tempted like as we are, yet
without sin.   Let us therefore come boldly unto the
throne of grace, that we may obtain mercy, and find
grace to help in time of need."

Because there is not a Christian here but knows
how resolutely he has to confront such thoughts as
these : " I am not worthy.   Who am I ?   A poor
worm."   But we have an High Priest who can be
touched with the feeling of our infirmities, and
who has now passed into the heavens.   How
wonderful is the thought suggested by these words.

Shall you and I see the glory of God? How? By virtue of the High Priest. He has offered Himself. While you and I exercise faith in Him, we are transformed by the Spirit of the living God. And thus this fourth chapter closes, speaking to us in words of distinguishing power; for, indeed, the Word is ointment to bind up the broken heart.

Whom have you in the fifth chapter introduced? You have Aaron. You see Moses has come; Joshua has come; the Land has come; the Sabbath has come — at first God's rest from creation; now it means our rest on account of redemption; it is perpetual rest. We keep perpetual Sabbath from January 1st to December 31st, enchanted with the glory that is in us. There remaineth a rest to the people of God, for we are looking for the glory and finished work of Christ.

And in this fifth chapter, you will find not only Aaron referred to, but you will find also Melchisedek. Why? Because God made Aaron a priest forever after the order of Melchisedek. Melchisedek suddenly appeared on the scene, and was recognized by Abraham as God's priest. And Christ is a priest forever. He is no after-thought of God. God has followed Him up, as it were, through the ages. In the seventh chapter, twenty-third and twenty-fourth verses we read:

"And they truly were many priests, because they were not suffered to continue by reason of death: but this man, because he continueth ever, hath an unchangeable priesthood."

The death of Jesus Christ becomes the ground-
work of His everlasting priesthood.   Melchisedek
hides himself and is gone, and Christ stands alone.

" I other priests disdain, and laws and off'rings too ;
        None but the bleeding Lamb, the mighty work can do."

In the eighth chapter, you will find that the
apostle refers to the olden covenant.   Be reminded
of this fact, that the olden covenant was not perfect,
because it was weak through the flesh ; but the
days have come when Christ shall establish the
new.   Under the law there was continually the
remembrance of sin.   Under the law it is written :
"Cursed is every one that continueth not in all
things which are written in the book of the law to
do them."   Under the Gospel it is written, " I will
be merciful to their unrighteousness, and their sins
and their iniquities will I remember no more."
Now, in the ninth chapter, blessed be God, we still
go back into the history of the past, and we read
these words :

"Then verily the first covenant had also ordinances of
divine service, and a worldly sanctuary.   For there was a
tabernacle made ; the first wherein was the candlestick,
and the table, and the shew-bread ; which is called the
sanctuary.   And after the second vail, the tabernacle
which is called the Holiest of all."

Here the tabernacle speaks the name of Christ.
The candlestick says, ' I was but a type of Him
who is the Light of the world ; ' the table of shew-
bread says, ' I did but speak of Him who came
down from heaven, and is the Bread of Life.'   In

the holiest of all, we find the golden censer, the golden pot of manna, Aaron's rod that budded, the tables of the law, and the Ark of the Covenant, where was the place of promised blessing. "There will I meet with thee and commune with thee." In that ark you know were placed those two tables of stone, and the mercy seat covered the law. Christ and His word must be removed out of the way before any soul that trusts in Him can receive the condemnation of the law.

The apostle refers to the offerings in the service, of which every bullock speaks of Christ ; every goat speaks of Christ, and every lamb speaks of the Lamb which taketh away the sins of the world. All have one testimony ; they speak of Christ.

"For if the blood of bulls and of goats, and the ashes of an heifer sprinkling the unclean, sanctifieth to the purifying of the flesh : how much more shall the blood of Christ who through the eternal Spirit offered himself without spot to God, purge your conscience from dead works to serve the living God ? "

And then we have previous testimony concerning the Testator :

"And for this cause he is the mediator of the new testament, that by means of death, for the redemption of the transgressions that were under the first testament, they which are called might receive the promise of eternal inheritance."

If you want to know what you are worth to-day, go and look at the will of your God. " A testament

is in force after men are dead ; " and Christ has
died, and when I want to know what I am worth, I
go and turn over His precious will. The chapter
closes, and here again the platform is clear and
Christ stands alone.

"And as it is appointed unto men once to die, but after
this the judgment : so Christ was once offered to bear the
sins of many ; and unto them that look for him shall he
appear the second time without sin unto salvation.   For
the law having a shadow of good things to come, and
not the very image of the things, can never with those
sacrifices which they offered year by year continually,
make the comers thereunto perfect.   For then would
they not have ceased to be offered ? because that the worshipers once purged should have had no more conscience
of sins.   But in those sacrifices there is a remembrance
again made of sins every year.   For it is not possible
that the blood of bulls and of goats should take away
sins.   Wherefore, when he cometh into the world, he
saith, Sacrifice and offering thou wouldest not, but a
body hast thou prepared me : in burnt-offerings and
sacrifices for sin thou hast had no pleasure.   Then said
I, Lo, I come (in the volume of the book it is written
of me,) to do thy will, O God. "

Christ Jesus comes, born of a woman, unto us,
so that we can say He is part of our body, our
flesh, our bones ; and we are His.   Oh the blessedness of a union with Christ.   He has lifted us up
from being worms to being princes with God.
Sons and daughters of the living God !   That law
which was against us, He has taken out of the way
and nailed to the cross.   And now there comes a
solemn warning :

"He that despised Moses' law, died without mercy under two or three witnesses: of how much sorer punishment, suppose ye, shall he be thought worthy, who hath trodden under foot the Son of God, and hath counted the blood of the covenant, wherewith he was sanctified, an unholy thing, and hath done despite unto the Spirit of grace?"

My sister, I could weep over you, when I find you taken up with trifles instead of Christ. My brother, my heart is full of sorrow, when I see you drawing together trifles light as air, and meanwhile selling your birthright. Many of you are loving sin. You think if you were to receive Christ, you would be a loser. Many thousands of young hearts have this black, horrid thought, that if they were to receive Christ, they would be plunged into poverty. Let a blind man who has recovered his sight burst into tears ; that would be reasonable ; but that the heart should refuse Christ through fear of diminished happiness is fearful.

How beautifully does the eleventh chapter open :

"Now faith is the substance of things hoped for, the evidence of things not seen. For by it the elders obtained a good report. Through faith we understand that the worlds were framed by the word of God, so that things which are seen were not made of things which do appear."

Now, observe, we have a different kind of testimony. We have just finished with the Mosaic economy. We have had the law saying, "I was but a shadow." Now all creation comes and says,

" We declare Christ unto you." Every star speaks
to us of Him who was revealed to the wise men by
a star. The sun says, " I speak to you of the Sun
of righteousness which has arisen with healing in
His wings." Yonder blue vault of heaven speaks
of the lustre of the house to which He is gathering
His people. Now we go right back to Abel. He
comes with his slaughtered lamb, and pointing to
Christ, he says, " That is why I did not choose my
brother's kind of offering. I heard God say, 'Without the shedding of blood is no remission of sins.'"
And so he took the type of the Lamb of God.

And next to Abel comes Enoch. He " walked
with God : and he was not ; for God took him."
He says, " Christ was my life ; and it was from
Him I received the testimony that I pleased Him,
and He took me home." And when Enoch is
gone, Noah comes with his ark, every timber of
which speaks of Christ. The storm overwhelms
all without, but all is safe within. The higher the
waters of judgment rise, the nearer do they bear
the vessel to its home.

Abraham, when called to go into a place which
he should after receive for an inheritance, went
out, not knowing whither. And he says, I did this,
because I wished to witness for Christ : " For he
looked for a city which hath foundations, whose
builder and maker is God." The voice of Sarah
too is heard in the long line of illustrious ones who
believe, " because she judged Him faithful who had
promised." And so they all come trooping to this
platform, bearing testimony to Christ.

Thus this chapter finishes speaking to us in these glorious words : " And these all, having obtained a good report through faith, received not the promise : God having provided some better thing for us, that they without us should not be made perfect." They all looked unto Jesus, the author and finisher of their faith. See to it, that your eye be upon Him. You and I are united to Him, soon to be acknowledged as His, very likely before we ever have a chance to meet again. Walk worthy of the high vocation wherewith God doth call you, the loins of your mind being girded with truth.

"Wherefore, seeing we also are compassed about with so great a cloud of witnesses, let us lay aside every weight, and the sin which doth so easily beset us, and let us run with patience the race that is set before us, looking unto Jesus the author and finisher of our faith ; who, for the joy that was set before him, endured the cross, despising the shame, and is set down at the right hand of the throne of God. For consider him that endured such contradiction of sinners against himself, lest ye be wearied and faint in your minds. Ye have not yet resisted unto blood, striving against sin. And ye have forgotten the exhortation which speaketh unto you as unto children, My son, despise not thou the chastening of the Lord, nor faint when thou art rebuked of him : for whom the Lord loveth he chasteneth, and scourgeth every son whom he receiveth. If ye endure chastening, God dealeth with you as with sons ; for what son is he whom the father chasteneth not ? But if ye be without chastisement, whereof all are partakers, then are ye bastards, and not sons."

Does some poor suffering child of God say, "How little is my conscious experience like what you have portrayed!" Listen. He tells us not to be distressed by sorrow. You are chastened, are you? Well, "we have had fathers of our flesh which corrected us, and we gave them reverence." But our God sitteth as the refiner and purifier of silver. He never uses the amputating knife when the pruning knife will do.

Now, you are not come unto Mount Sinai, but ye are come unto Mount Zion. Remember, ye ARE come unto Zion; not ye shall come by and by, but you *are* come already. In more happiness, but not more secure, are the glorified spirits in heaven!

"Ye are come unto Mount Zion, and unto the city of the living God, the heavenly Jerusalem, and to an innumerable company of angels, to the general assembly and church of the first-born, which are written in heaven, and to God the Judge of all, and to the spirits of just men made perfect, and to Jesus the Mediator of the new covenant, and to the blood of sprinkling, that speaketh better things than that of Abel."

Therefore, in the first verse of the last chapter:

"Let brotherly love continue. Be not forgetful to entertain strangers; for thereby some have entertained angels unawares. Remember them that are in bonds, as bound with them; and them which suffer adversity, as being yourselves also in the body. Marriage is honorable in all, and the bed undefiled: but whoremongers and adulterers God will judge."

I ask you never to forget how God joins together the highest spiritual blessings with the most solemn warnings. "Marriage is honorable in all, and the bed undefiled : but whoremongers and adulterers God will judge." Why does God speak like this? Because He knows what man is.

"And walk in love, as Christ also hath loved us, and hath given himself for us an offering and a sacrifice to God for a sweet-smelling savor,"

is one verse.

"But fornication, and all uncleanness, or covetousness, let it not be once named among you, as becometh saints ; neither filthiness, nor foolish talking, nor jesting, which are not convenient : but rather giving of thanks. For this ye know, that no whoremonger, nor unclean person, nor covetous man, who is an idolater, hath any inheritance in the kingdom of Christ and of God,"

is the very next sentence. What God thus joins together, let us be very careful not to put asunder. Oh that you and I may have our feet upon the neck of appetite and passion, as Paul says :

"But I keep under my body, and bring it into subjection : lest that by any means when I have preached to others, I myself should be a cast-away."

"Jesus Christ, the same yesterday, and to-day, and for ever." There is no change in Him, nor in His teachings. You are not to be carried about with divers and strange doctrines. There are some things in this city which I dare not speak softly

about. Christ says, "Beware of the leaven of the
Pharisees."   The fact of false doctrine is worse
than that of drunkenness.   False teaching is en-
trenched in an impregnable fortress of the devil's
planting.

In the fifteenth verse, what have you and I to
do ? We have our sacrifice to offer.   It is very
beautiful.   It is the closing thought I give you, and
I pray you feed upon it until your souls rejoice.
" By Him therefore let us offer the sacrifice of
praise to God continually."   "Blessed are they that
dwell in Thy house : they will be still praising
Thee."   Our life should be a long thanksgiving
psalm of praise.   Praise God for the Son that put
away your sin ; praise Him for the cross that
brought you life ; praise Him for the power that
keeps you every moment, and is pledged to keep
you every moment until you stand in His presence ;
praise Him for all the blessings that flow to you
through Christ.   " By Him therefore let us offer
the sacrifice of praise to God continually, that is,
the fruit of our lips, giving thanks to His name."
Let us shout for joy in possession of Him through
whom all things are yours, for ye are in Christ and
He in you.   In possession of Him, the spirit of
poverty is cast out, for "there is therefore now no
condemnation to them which are in Christ Jesus,
who walk not after the flesh, but after the Spirit."
Oh, that to-day you may gather the deep, full
meaning of the words.   And now, I need not to
give a benediction here, for my Father gives it to
you :

"Now the God of peace, that brought again from the dead our Lord Jesus, that great Shepherd of the sheep, through the blood of the everlasting covenant, make you perfect in every good work, to do his will, working in you that which is well-pleasing in his sight, through Jesus Christ; to whom be glory for ever and ever. AMEN."

www.ingramcontent.com/pod-product-compliance
Lightning Source LLC
Chambersburg PA
CBHW020059030726
47498CB00006B/1860